YOU CEO

Success Lessons from Leading CEOs

VIKASH MITTERSAIN | CYRUS M. GONDA | NITIN PARAB

I0563734

EMBASSY BOOKS
www.embassybooks.in

YOU CEO

Published in India by :
EMBASSY BOOK DISTRIBUTORS
120, Great Western Building,
Maharashtra Chamber of Commerce Lane,
Fort, Mumbai - 400 023.
Tel : (+91-22) 22819546 / 32967415
Email : info@embassybooks.in
Website: www.embassybooks.in

Disclaimer : The information in this book has been taken from exclusive interviews with the professionals contained in this volume.
The position of each executive is reflected as on the date that the interview was taken.

ISBN : 978-93-85492-24-2

Printed in India by Repro India Pvt Ltd.

TABLE OF CONTENTS

YOU - CEO

PREFACE

If you need sound medical advice, you go to a renowned doctor or surgeon.

If you need good financial inputs, you approach a chartered accountant or a chartered financial analyst.

For the best legal advice, you would visit a solicitor or a senior counsel.

So logically, when inputs on what constitutes effective corporate leadership are needed, who best to go to than the most successful CEOs and corporate practitioners themselves?

We were fortunate to get direct access and exclusive interviews with nine stalwarts of Indian industry, men and a woman who are literally household names. They have often been interviewed on their personal success and how they lead their organisations.

But we met them with a different agenda in mind.

We wanted their specific inputs on what according to them constitutes sound corporate leadership, their views on the burning topic of corporate social responsibility, and most important of all, their take on what are the qualities an aspiring leader should focus on if he wishes to take his place among the corporate greats in the near future.

They gave of their experiences freely and generously, and we have culled, extracted and collated the best of what they had to say. It is presented for you here in ready form, like a 'Leadership Bible.'

Our country is blessed with all possible resources except the crucial one of effective leadership, which is why we witness brain-drain – our best brains going overseas as they cannot function in the rudderless and aimless environment which is what we offer them.

Our objective is to create more leaders, especially in the corporate domain, and with the excellent and specific tips provided by the nine stalwarts we met, we hope to at last ensure that the next generation

of corporate aspirants and entrepreneurs can fulfill the leadership void which is the only genuine dearth our country faces.

Read this book with great care, read it over and over, mark out the parts which are of special interest to you, put into practice the parts you feel you need to work upon to improve your leadership quotient, and enjoy your ride to the top of whichever path you choose.

INTRODUCTION

C hange itself is changing, so rapid is its pace, and the world of business is going through a metamorphosis such as was never witnessed before.

Technology apparently being firmly in the driver's seat has made the future fascinating for many, but ultimately it is the people-centric organisations that are ideally positioned to sustain and create positive impact.

To understand the intricacies of the new-age phenomenon, we authors set out on a mission to unravel the hidden secrets of corporate success. In the journey to understand the business mindset of the future, we were fortunate to get exclusive interviews with the doyens of Indian Industry.

Having captured their thought processes for posterity, we were able to shape their thoughts and extract their keen insights to focus on providing a concentrated message for the readers who wish to emulate these legends and create leadership benchmarks of their own.

With the help of these inputs took shape this book that offers productive and profitable insights on some of the most practical and fundamental leadership and managerial principles such as:

- Clarity of goals and formulation of vision
- Identification and nurturing of best talent
- Training and developing skills essential to harness technological advances
- Obtaining and providing constructive feedback
- Establishing a culture of innovation
- Building trust and fostering loyalty
- Energising people through the communication of vision and purpose

Meeting and interviewing these leaders, who each expressed their thoughts in such a candid and transparent manner, was in itself a life-enriching experience.

The objective of creating this book was to charter the evolving thought process of successful corporate leaders who have built their business empire through recognising the potential of their people, establishing a transparent communication system, and nurturing an environment which motivates their workforce to achieve extraordinary levels of productivity. They have also been able to successfully adapt their own behaviour to attune with different people, situations and circumstances, thereby establishing the hallmark of true leadership.

We also captured their thrust on the aspect of corporate social responsibility, a term which has become the corporate buzzword with the incorporation of the India's new Companies Act - 2013.

We firmly believe that the future of business will largely depend on the strength of the personal branding of the leader, coupled with what values his/her company stands for. How organisations will respond to crisis, how organisations will leverage their uniqueness to fill in a void in the market place, and how organizations will innovate their systems and processes to strategise themselves and thus stay a step ahead in the competitive world – these are the challenges that tomorrow's leadership needs to be geared up for.

As the corporate world and its leaders come under increasing scrutiny, it is this very scrutiny which will enforce organisations to build a sustainable future upon the trust factor. Trust and the power of strong relationships, built upon the foundation of eternal values, will be the edifice on which the future enterprise will stand firm.

We are positive that the deep learning from our experience in interacting with these nine legends is similarly felt by our readers, and they in turn will get inspired to take on the challenges and opportunities that will be ushered in by the 'New Age.'

And before you commence reading this section and the rest of this book, we would like you to ponder upon the immortal lines of the poet Henry Wadsworth Longfellow:

Lives of great men all remind us,

We can make our lives sublime,

And, departing, leave behind us,

Footprints on the sands of time.

THE SELECTION PROCESS

A very relevant question may crop up in the mind of our readers – **WHY** did we select **THESE** nine CEOs for our book on leadership?

Simply because they represent the very best for the structured approach we adopted for this book.

Within the limit of nine very senior corporate leaders we had set for ourselves, we wanted to get the best individuals from the widest variety of backgrounds with the common thread of leadership excellence.

The wide variety of backgrounds was essential to understand how leadership emerges and leadership thought processes are defined when CEOs attain mastery over their domain after arriving at it from diverse backgrounds – such as carrying an existing family business forward to greater heights, or being a first-mover and building an entire industry from scratch, or being a professional career CEO from a western background and then taking up a senior assignment in India, or being of Indian origin but developing a business empire overseas, or being a mentor to CEOs by deriving leadership insights through captaincy in cricket – which is almost akin to a religion in India.

Keeping these parameters in mind so that our readers could get a holistic flavour of leadership from diverse perspectives, we chose the best nine leaders possible. They are:

- Taking existing family business forward to greater heights (consolidation and expansion) through superb blend of qualifications and experience – **Nadir Godrej** (Godrej Indistries), **Ajay Piramal** (Piramal Group) and **Anu Aga** (Thermax)

- Building up entire industries from scratch with the power of knowledge and vision – **Dr Kanodia** (first CEO of TCS and founder of IT industry in India) and **Dr Subhash Chandra** (founder of television programming and broadcasting in India)

- Professional CEOs of foreign origin heading multinational brands in Indian environment – **Marten Pieters** (Vodafone India) and **Martin Kriegner** (Lafarge India)

- CEO of Indian origin operating overseas – **Ramesh Hira** (R Hira Group)

- A trainer to CEOs on the subject of mastering leadership through the sport of cricket – Ayaz Memon

Hoping you as readers derive as much pleasure and learning from reading their insights as we did when we interviewed them in person.

THE BIRTH OF CEO

The **CHIEF EXECUTIVE OFFICER** is like a Master Surfer, surfing on the Tidal Waves of Change. He needs to balance his act skillfully as the unruly waves constantly rise up to knock him under. But by developing a perfectly aligned body which is in tune with the mind, he should learn to gracefully ride the waves, appearing in full control of the shark-infested ocean surrounding him.

In this world plagued with unpredictability, the CEO needs to develop a very high sense of the following:

- Understanding of his inner self, the knowledge of his personal weaknesses and strengths

- Understanding that business cannot be run on whimsical or self-centric grounds, and that he needs to establish the core team through which decisions are deliberated, enacted and monitored

- A clear perspective on how the markets are shifting and an understanding of behavioural patterns in business

- An eagle eye on the emerging trends in technology as well as trends in other domains

Concurrent Change is taking place and the New Age CEO should emerge as the Change Champion.

He not only needs to be prepared but he should always be in a state of constant preparation. Prepared to be nimble footed to take swift decisions, tweak his business model, see the tsunami of change coming and alter the course, and most importantly to be in constant communication with his workforce and the external eco-sphere within which he and his organisation operates.

Dear reader, we believe that you are already a CEO or an aspirational CEO in the making. However large or small your enterprise is, this book will give you deep insights to prepare your mind to face the adventure of your business life with clarity and courage.

The journey ahead is littered with umpteen opportunities, and this book will provide you with the picture of a Modern Day CEO, which once imprinted in your inner mind, will provide you with the strength and substance to forge your way forward. Through these pages, you will be treated to a feast of deep intellectual insights of the great CEOs who have been interviewed at length and who parted with their practical wisdom on how they manage their present organisations and how they have made them future-centric.

There are nine greats who grace the cover and pages of this book – nine greats who we have been fortunate enough to interview exclusively, and who have offered and shared their innermost secrets which will enable you to understand **HOW** to replicate and acquire the qualities which they state are the most important for you to reach the CEO pinnacle. They have created the path – you need to follow in their footsteps, making your own additions to the path along the way.

The term 'CEO' is relatively new and may have been around for less than a hundred years. The initial title was that of 'Super Manager' and it was associated with organisations in the west which were rapidly expanding and growing due to the impetus of the Industrial revolution. Especially in the U.S., we learned that it became difficult for family-business owners to manage the stupendous growth that came their way, and therefore they brought in these Super Managers to look after the strategy, policy making, operational aspects, administration, marketing and financial aspects of the company which had become increasingly complex. The Super Manager not only managed the business, but ensured its sustained growth, both nationally and internationally.

In due course of time, the Super Manager started harnessing the skills needed by a leader, thereby taking ownership of business operations. Thus was born the term CEO or the Chief Operating Officer. The CEO could either be the founder/owner or could be a professionally appointed individual. The CEO would report to the Board of Directors and would ultimately be responsible for all aspects of functioning within the company. Subsequently, similar high level positions came into existence such as CMO (Chief Marketing Officer), CIO (Chief Information Officer), CTO (Chief Technology Officer), and so on.

The CEO literally ruled his organisation and corporate history is full of how these men and women left a lasting legacy or how they brought their organisation to dust.

In India, the title CEO is of comparable recent vintage. It is in the last 15 years or so that the word CEO became commonplace. The trend in India in this context was started by Americanised Indian companies, especially those in the domain of software and technology. The title is more of a status symbol rather than a legal requirement. (India recognizes the title 'Managing Director' as the final legally responsible person within an organisation when the legality issue arises.)

Why indeed do we need a professional CEO in the first place?

The founders/owners of organisations, especially in western countries, who started small but grew large due to the excellence of their product or service offering, found that they did not personally possess the depth of relevant expertise and the bandwidth of talent to handle the complexities demanded by a large growing business. They adapted to the situation by bringing in professionals to run their companies. This gave rise to what came to be known as the 'C-Suite.'

In the Indian context we have the benefit of learning from the developments made in the west and leap-frogging into the latest management techniques and expertise. We in India did not go through the pains of restructuring our business models the way the west went about working over the past so many decades. Thus we in India today are happily on par or on an equal footing with corporate leaders across the globe.

As you go through this book, you will realise that India as a country is uniquely poised to take corporate center stage. We have the youngest nation status, and with the GDP projected to grow in double digits, India has emerged among the foremost nations of the world. In the next five year India will transform and will be rubbing shoulders with the super powers. Business in India will undergo a drastic transformation. Against this backdrop, the leader's mindset will create the New Age CEO.

This CEO will require to acquire 'New Age Skills' such as:

- Understand relatively where he stands in the corporate eco-system and how he can best position his business idea

- Rise through an apprentice-modeled education and learning so that through observation and the guidance of his mentor, he is able to understand the ethos of business creation

- Should be able to motivate himself and his people and understand the science of self-energising

- Most important, the CEO needs to have a robust and energetic entrepreneurial mindset

Some attributes which the 'New Age CEO' needs to focus upon and develop are listed below:

- Should possess an ambitious nature and inner drive

- Should be able to synchronise his personal brand with the organisation's brand

- Should be able to take calculated risks

- Should be able to read the customers' mindset and create a customer-centric organisation

- Should be achievement oriented

- Should be primarily dedicated to achieve the organisational goals

- Should be able to effectively communicate the company vision across the workforce

- Needs to have a 'never-say-die' attitude

- Finally, the 'New Age CEO' should possess cultural Intelligence and should be capable of making the world his workplace

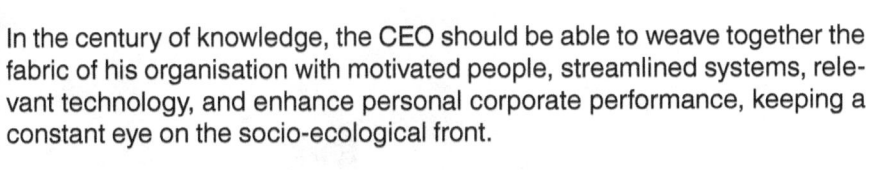

In the century of knowledge, the CEO should be able to weave together the fabric of his organisation with motivated people, streamlined systems, relevant technology, and enhance personal corporate performance, keeping a constant eye on the socio-ecological front.

We wish you all the best on your leadership journey, and are sure you will find the insights provided by the legendary CEOs we have interviewed extremely helpful to reach your chosen destination.

NADIR
GODREJ

MANAGING DIRECTOR

> **" *I firmly believe that the power of strategic thinking should be spread throughout the organisation* "**
>
> -Nadir Godrej

The word **STRATEGIOS** is of Greek origin, coined many, many centuries ago, and it signifies the 'coming together of people for a common purpose or a common objective.'

Strategy can be viewed, studied, and practiced from the levels of its three component elements:

- Strategic Thought
- Strategic Plan
- Strategic Action

These three need to go in sync and sequence so that organisations can positively differentiate and position themselves in a competitive environment.

NADIR **GODREJ**, Managing Director of Godrej Industries, is **one of the most highly qualified top executives in India.**

A student of St. Xavier's school and college, Mumbai, he then went on to secure his:

Bachelor of Chemical Engineering from the Massachusetts Institute of Technology (MIT)

Master of Chemical Engineering from Stanford University

MBA from the Harvard Business School....

......all three ranked among the very top institutes in the U.S.A.

We were indeed privileged to spend quality time with him and gained immensely from his invaluable insights on the topics of leadership, corporate branding, and social responsibility.

4

A WELL ROUNDED PERSONALITY

M r. Godrej, apart from his phenomenal academic accomplishments, is also a poet at heart, a mentor by choice, a leader by profession, a very humble person by nature, and believes in the power of collaborative leadership.

He loves playing chess, bridge and Scrabble; all games that inculcate strategic thinking and sharpen recall.

He speaks six languages, including Russian and French.

Nadir Godrej leads his organisation with the strength of clarity and a thoughtful, tactical mind. As mentioned, not only is he the MD of the Godrej Industries - soaps and consumer products division, but also the Chairman of Godrej Agrovet – the agrochemicals division.

TOP TO BOTTOM
-BOTTOM TO TOP

A ccording to him, leadership comes not necessarily from the top. He feels it is a highly collaborative approach. The entire strategy team at Godrej gets involved in developing the organisational strategic process. They have a strategy department that constantly looks out onto what the world is doing, what is likely to evolve, the impact of these changes on business, and other factors. This team then develops and fine-tunes strategies, and if found feasible, the new strategy then goes to market.

Nadir Godrej firmly believes that the power of strategic thinking is spread throughout the organisation. Ideas are everywhere. In the organisational context ideas percolate upwards; they are then consolidated and then deployed to the appropriate channel, where they can be most profitably used.

The best ideas come from the grassroots; from the front-line people who have felt the pulse of the market, who are in touch with and who know the reality of the vast world which lies beyond the narrow organisational boundaries. It is the front-line people in any organisation who are in sync with the thought processes of customers and prospects which are ever-changing. The top management constantly needs to solicit feedback from these front-end staff who are an invaluable source of information.

Feedback, according to him, is critical and ought to be a two-way exchange of thought.

TO DIVERSIFY OR NOT?
-THAT IS THE QUESTION

When it comes to the question of determining the levels of diversification which a business house should explore, Mr. Godrej believes that **it is always easier to be in your core business** because of the competency in-built in your area of expertise over the ages. But the problem arises when some of your existing businesses which have formed the bread-and-butter of your balance sheet may no longer be relevant to the times. So if there is a good strategic reason to start a new business, one could look at that.

However, he advises that one should **never underestimate the challenge of moving into a new business area.** First do your homework and research very thoroughly, and then if you find the option to be strategically feasible, only then should it be stepped into.

At Godrej, he says, they love to **experiment**. Often. To find new methods and new pathways. Strategically, changes have often been attempted. Some succeed, some do not.

An example he provides is that of Godrej Consumer Products. It was a company which initially operated solely in the Indian domestic market, but an opportunistic acquisition in the U.K. made them go international. Further the U.K. company received an acquisition opportunity in South Africa, and this then led to a conscious strategy to look for businesses in other developing markets across the globe. So a bit of **serendipity and good fortune** and also some **experimentation** based on **evidence**, ultimately resulted in a profitable strategic move.

THRUST ON TRAINING

An area which Nadir Godrej in his role as a leader is passionate about and firmly believes in is the function of **Training and Development**. This is an important activity which his organisation substantially invests in. He believes that **India currently has a large training-knowledge gap**, but the **good thing is that it is quite easy to impart training as our people are eager and willing to learn and enhance their skill-sets**.

At Godrej, they have an **in-house MBA programme**, in which they have partnered with various business schools. This is an on-site programme on the company premises, so the employees don't have to commute to college. The classes are conducted after office hours, so the company does not lose on working-time, and the interested employees get an opportunity to strengthen their formal qualifications.

The course and the curriculum are customised and tailor-made for the employees and designed to accommodate the needs of the organisation. The **training is intelligently integrated with the job requirements and needs of the organisation** and it has thus resulted into a win-win situation.

Mr. Godrej also observes and compares the **skills-gap** he identifies in other industries, and feels that at Godrej, this gap is comparatively not so large. They have moderately skilled people already available and also do not find it difficult to source skilled people. If there is the need for a certain skill-set that can be developed in-house, **they impart it to the employees through the appropriate training measures**.

LEAD BY DELEGATING

A strong factor in their success story is the motivated and dedicated workforce which exists in Godrej Industries due to the scientific recruitment process which is firmly in place.

The recruitment process itself is handled by capable people and Mr. Godrej does not play a strong role in it, thus displaying his important leadership quality of delegation and having faith in subordinates to do crucial jobs well.

THE GENESIS OF GODREJ

Coming to the commencement of the organisation itself, Godrej as a business entity was born in 1897, started by Nadir Godrej's grand-uncle, with their first business being the manufacturing of **surgical instruments**. But that business was not successful and is no longer part of the organisation's offerings. Then came the famous Godrej **locks**, which strengthened their brand-name and built them a **reputation for quality**, and then locks became the foundation for their engineering business, which is now known as Godrej & Boyce.

His grand-uncle was an enterprising gentleman, and apart from initiating the surgical instruments division, also commenced making **soaps from vegetable oils**. This was a first for India, as till that time, soap was made primarily in the unorganised sector and with animal fats. **Thus Godrej can be credited with introducing the first vegetarian soap for the Indian consumer.**

A SPIRIT OF PATRIOTISM

The other business which was started by this pioneering individual was the manufacturing of **fire-proof safes**. The grand-uncle was not a scientist nor was he a mechanically-qualified man, but **developed this business by reading the right books on the subject**. This is a fine lesson for the youth of today, and demonstrates **how much can be achieved in life by the simple act of appropriate reading**. Nadir Godrej adds that his grand-uncle was initially a lawyer by profession, but gave up his practice after arguing one last case in Zanzibar (now part of modern-day Tanzania). He had to lie to win the case and thus decided that the practice of law was not suitable for him.

He (Nadir's grand-uncle) had even met Mahatma Gandhi (both had been born in the same year), and told him, that he (Gandhi) talked of independent India, but the country had no economy, so how could it be **economically independent**. Gandhi then asked him in turn, "So if that is the case, what are **you** doing about it." And that was the **start of the patriotic Godrej story**.

Nadir's grand-uncle was 12 years older than Nadir's grandfather. The grand-uncle sold one business to Nadir's grandfather and the soaps business was donated to the Parsi Panchayat (a Charitable Trust). Under the Trust, it went bankrupt, and was bought back by his grandfather.

Thus Nadir Godrej emphasises that both the initial businesses were ultimately bought by his grandfather and were not inherited. Nadir's father was the second generation and he passed away in 1994.

11

DO WHAT YOU **LOVE** TO DO

Mr. Nadir Godrej is the third generation of this renowned business family. And the   fourth generation is well on its way to taking over the reins in due course.

Nadir Godrej's eldest son is graduating in earth systems, with a specialisation in agriculture and planet climate change, and has interned at Godrej. His second son has also interned with the organisation. His youngest son is interested in neuro-science, and as of now does not want to join the family business. Though he is very entrepreneurial by nature; he may want to start his own business in his area of interest.

Nadir Godrej does not want to influence the career paths or future choices of any of his sons, and will leave it up to them to whether to join the business or make their mark elsewhere. The choice is theirs.

'MAKE IN INDIA' IS OUR MANTRA

Godrej is primarily a manufacturing business, and fits in well with Prime Minister Narendra Modi's **'MAKE IN INDIA'** campaign.

LEARN FROM THE JAPANESE

Mr. Godrej also feels **that his organisation has learned a lot from the Japanese** – in areas like Improvement processes, Kaizen, Total Productivity Management, Total Quality Management, and many other pioneering Japanese management and leadership practices.

The understanding and introduction of these techniques has also led to tremendous improvements in management-labour relationships. He recalls how on one occasion in the past their workers had gone on strike under a communist union, but the management had kept the operations running with managers, officers and even Godrej family-members coming and running the factory. But with the introduction of Japanese management techniques (which are very employee-oriented), labour relations have dramatically improved, and they haven't had a strike since then.

CHINA MAY WIN ON COST – BUT INDIA CAN WIN ON QUALITY

He observes that China has the advantage of having the ability to be flexible and fast in designing and manufacturing products, a factor which has strengthened the Chinese economy. It is the 'qual-cost' factor, (i.e. quality at a reasonable cost), which leads to products being offered by China at an affordable price. Mr. Nadir Godrej is of the firm belief that India can compete on this parameter also. With better technology and skills available to us, India too can make globally acceptable products.

He very insightfully mentions: **"Our strength lies not in cheap labour, but in low cost engineers. We have our expertise in the engineering industry, pharmaceuticals industry, speciality chemical industry; even in the manufacture of auto-parts we are very successful. Our overall labour cost may be higher than China's; which is why they beat us on cost, but not on quality."**

RETAIN TALENT – CREATE A
CONDUCIVE WORKING ENVIRONMENT

He says that many businesspeople often complain that engineers leave organisations in search of greener pastures; but to **retain** them, **the onus lies with the organisations. People leave organisations for more money and enhanced job satisfaction**. If they are **compensated adequately and given interesting and challenging work**, then it bodes well for the company and the employee. This is the key to retaining valuable talent, which today is worth its weight in gold.

He admits there may be a little aversion by some engineers to working on the shop-floor, but if these engineers are creative and talented, it would be advantageous to place them in **Research & Development** and related functions where their knowledge and expertise can be put to effective use. Ultimately, he opines, the onus lies on the management to make the **workplace more attractive**.

He observes that in Information Technology companies, the atmosphere and mood is very similar to that of a university campus; the environment is vibrant. Whereas in a manufacturing organisation, engineers are made to work long hours and in relatively poor working conditions. Since such is the perception and often the case in reality, he rightly believes that manufacturing units need to make their workplaces more vibrant and people-oriented to attract and retain the best talent.

After all, as he says, **for an organisation, its people are the true differentiators**.

THE QUALITIES A LEADER NEEDS TO DEVELOP

N adir Godrej is a CEO who has many CEOs reporting to him. As such, he can be considered a CEO of CEOs.

When asked about the **qualities that a CEO should possess,** he feels the most important is the **ability to carry people along with them.** A CEO should have a good '**Command Model**' as a CEO needs to carry a lot of people along the path to organisational success.

Also, he feels the CEO should be **futuristic.** He should be able to foresee and **envision the future.**

A CEO also needs to ensure that **people are treated well** and not like robots. **Discipline is necessary,** but you need to carry people along with you willingly. A leader needs to develop **cognitive intelligence** as well as **emotional intelligence.**

A CEO need not be an expert number cruncher, but he needs to be able to **understand the importance of numbers,** and **understand numbers.** That, along with the ability to carry people along is all that is necessary to succeed.

GIVE 'PSYCHOLOGY'
THE IMPORTANCE THAT IT DESERVES

Unfortunately, Mr. Nadir Godrej feels that emotional intelligence is not taught as a separate subject in most business schools.

Psychology as a science is also often not given the importance it rightly deserves at the higher education level.

Relating this to the management within his organisation, he recalls that Godrej was earlier run mainly by engineers; but that is changing now. They are looking at individuals from other disciplines too, to play leadership roles.

FOCUS ON CULTURE – IT GIVES GOOD DIVIDENDS

The **Godrej Cultural Centre** at their Vikhroli complex in Mumbai has made the complex a vibrant place.

There is some cultural event or the other organised every Friday evening – either a lecture, a movie (documentaries, not commercial movies), discussions and debates on topics of general or special interest, etc.

All this leads to a **wider exchange of ideas**, and he is happy that this involvement and exchange of **cultural thought-processes has positively impacted the function of marketing and also improved the ability of his employees in dealing with people.**

BACK TO CAMPUS

Another initiative taken by the Human Resources function at their organisation is the priority given to recruiting for jobs from among those who have already been Summer Interns with the organisation in the past. This is a win-win situation for both the candidates as well as the organisation, as the interns already know the organisational systems and processes, and are familiar with the culture and the environment. Campus placements have been made smoother with this concept of hiring summer interns.

Godrej also recently conducted a unique contest on the subject of L.O.U.D. **'Live Out Ur Dreams'** as a creative method for campus placement recruitment. They resorted to this creative venture and not the standard, usual, 'business-plan' contest, and it gave them great results. The contest resulted in some interesting ideas from the participants. Some wrote that they wanted to go on an interesting holiday, some dreams were related to the hot-topic of CSR, some were related to music.

Mr. Godrej says, "We read all the entries and even funded some of them which we found worthy and thus helped fulfil a few dreams. What is more important is that through this process, we were able to evaluate the **emotional quotient** (EQ) of the participants and identify people with a good EQ. This helped us get a **good connect** and the question of needing to command or discipline them when they ultimately become part of our team does not arise. **When you have recruited people who are engaged and empowered, commitment comes in naturally."**

ENGAGEMENT LEADS TO COMMITMENT

P eople need to feel engaged to feel commitment to their organisation, and it is the duty of the organisation to look after the physical and emotional needs of the employees.

He feels a great example in this regard is the organisation 'Google.' Google has provided comfortable nap rooms, shower rooms, music rooms, entertainment rooms, exercise rooms, dining rooms; in short everything which makes an employee feel comfortable and at home.

It is not surprising that people do not mind working there even for 24 hours at a stretch.

One needs to give employees a free hand in doing the things they ought to do, work-wise.

In this regard, too, Mr Godrej says **"Our management lets the people work on projects largely conceptualised and developed by themselves, for the betterment of the organisation.** We have found that this empowerment of people engages them a lot in their work and leads to quality output. With this positive approach being adopted, we have found that we do not need to focus on negative approaches like punitive disciplining. **People are creative when left on their own. You then get engagement and commitment, and a resourcefulness that is unparalleled."**

SHARED VALUE

Godrej as a company does not believe in the traditional model of Corporate Social Responsibility (CSR). Rather, they have what is termed a '**Shared Values Concept**' as pioneered by Prof. Michael Porter.

They focus largely on 'green' and environment friendly projects and providing skills training, and this is not restricted only to their employees alone. They train beauticians, welders, appliance-repair persons, persons engaged in agriculture, and in many other diverse fields. These individuals and the professions they represent may or may not be related to the company. Godrej also works along with NGOs and with the marginalised sections of society, **to make them ready for employment, as they strongly believe that it is such skill-strength imparting which leads to people being able to stand on their own feet and become valuable members of society**.

As far as the concept of CSR goes, at Godrej Agrovet, apart from training they also focus strongly on **watershed development**, engaging in this along with an NGO that spearheads watershed development and management. Watershed development helps increase the price and value of the land on which it is done, and as a result, everyone benefits – the farmers, the land itself becomes more fertile, and also the climate in the area improves over a period of time.

This 'Shared Values Model' is the guiding-force of activities that ensures the company channelises its pathway into a socially responsible direction.

GO GREEN AND GROW

The focus and thrust in preserving the environment was started by Nadir's Uncle, Mr. Sorabjii Godrej.

Nadir's generation has donated The **Sohrabjii Godrej CII Green Centre building** in Hyderabad in his memory. This is also the first 'Platinum Lead' building in India. It does not need or have air-conditioning even in this city which has a warm climate, but is **cooled with natural air-conditioning**. It has a wind tower.

In fact, it is the Godrej Group which has spearheaded the concept of 'Green' and environmental-friendly technology in India.

This focus on the environment, apart from being socially responsible, has led to **large cost savings through affordable green energy.**

ALWAYS KEEP AN EYE OPEN FOR OPPORTUNITIES

T alking about Godrej Agrovet, he says it was a division of Godrej Soaps. They stumbled into this business quite by accident, once again **through serendipity, not strategy**, as he puts it. The story behind this business goes that Larsen & Toubro were in a business to produce animal feed plants which was a good venture, but they found they could not sell the product, and so asked us at Godrej to help them with the marketing of it, as we were already in the business of solvent-extraction. Since the factory was being offered at a reasonable price, we took it over and entered into the business. **Thus proving that one needs to keep an eye open for any opportunity that comes one's way.**

This is the story of how in 1973, Godrej entered into animal feed. In 1976 Nadir joined the business and took forward the animal feed business. Then they started making agro-chemicals, or biological agri-chemicals, which was the by-product of oil. To use neem oil in soap, it was necessary to remove all the natural chemicals that gave neem its smell, and many of these chemicals had insecticidal properties, so that led them into the business of natural insecticides and urea coating agents. They later developed plant growth promoters also from vegetable oils.

Thus it often happens that success in one business often leads to the development of a new opportunity in-house, which should be capitalised on.

THINK GLOBAL – ACT LOCAL

Nadir's view on emerging markets? He says that currently, only one of their businesses is truly global – Godrej Consumer Products (GCP). But the focus of the organisation is on markets in developing nations, which is where the future lies. Other than China and a few South-East Asian countries, they are well-entrenched in almost all developing nations. For example in Indonesia, Godrej has a huge presence.

Godrej as an organisation is also comfortable in dealing with various diverse cultures and has found their foray into diversity to be a success story so far. They believe in hiring local management to manage the work-force in whichever countries they operate in, and often the CEO is a local person as well. In Indonesia and in the U.K., they have Indians overseeing the Godrej operations, and the U.K. office also overlooks the Godrej businesses in Latin America. In these markets, they have not used global brands, but domestic brands. This is their strategy. To **use their own brands**. In South Africa they used local brands for the ethnic hair colour market, and Indian brands for the Caucasian market. The local brands there were not addressing the local Caucasian market and since Godrej was strong in this sector, they used the Godrej brand for the Caucasian market. They used the Indian brands to address the racially intermediate markets.

But for household insecticides, where there is no original brand available, they use the Godrej name. Brands like 'Hit' and 'Goodnight' were originally acquired, and are sold under their own name, under the umbrella of Godrej. **Thus there is deep thought that goes into all these activities, and nothing is arbitrary or left to chance.**

Godrej is a leading multinational in its areas of business, and as such Mr. Godrej believes the organisation should demonstrate a professional approach in all the markets it operates in. It is important that Indian companies are seen as forward and capable of being leaders at a global level.

THE ULTIMATE COMPLIMENT –
A **HARVARD** CASE STUDY ON GODREJ

And to conclude, a matter of great pride and something which demonstrates sufficient faith in the power of Indian management thoughts and practices is that **one of the professors at Harvard Business School has even interviewed Mr. Nadir Godrej for developing a management case-study on the business practices of the Godrej Group, especially the use of shared value**.

What greater honour could the world of management bestow on Mr. Nadir Godrej than this.

> **Feedback is critical and ought to always be a two-way exchange of thought**
>
> -Nadir Godrej

Leaders often believe that their role as far as **FEEDBACK** is concerned is restricted to providing it to those down the line. But for maximum impact, leaders need to be open to the concept of receiving feedback from their subordinates with regard to their policies, initiatives and other business related decisions.

In today's digital era, where e-commerce and e-business are in the driving seat, accurately and speedily gathering feedback from the entire business eco-system is crucial for survival and sustained growth.

Thus, being alert to context revives, reinforces and rejuvenates the product and service cycle of the organisation.

THE PRACTICALLY POETIC
TALENT OF MR.NADIR GODREJ

As mentioned previously, among the many other talents that Mr. Nadir Godrej possesses is the capacity for writing poetry – thoughtful and insightful poetry.

The following is an example of one of the poetic works he has penned, on a subject which is close to his heart – **Shared Value**.

We thank him for giving kind permission to reproduce it in our book.

SHARED VALUE – (A poem penned by Mr. Nadir Godrej)

Now there are those who would opine,
That businesses do just fine,
When business is all that they do.
To some extent this is true.
Just one objective is efficient.
And honest business seems sufficient
To help society at large.
And yet we're faced with the charge
That for want of a level playing field
The benefits that businesses yield
Accrue to the managerial class
While they bypass the toiling mass.
And hence was born CSR
And this can take us very far
But it entails a separation

Of the expenditure and generation
Of wealth. And yet we clearly know
No problem is solved by money flow
Alone. Some deep thought is required
For good solutions to be inspired.
And hence came this new paradigm.
Why did it take so much time?
Shared value makes a lot of sense
When viewed through a certain lens.
Now externalities are the base
On which one can make the case.
There is a conflict that we face
As we pursue the development race.
In many a developing nation
There is a lack of education.
We are then faced with climate change
And though it seems very strange
Governments can't decide
To take this problem in their stride.
If business goes on as before
These problems will hit us for sure.
So businesses themselves will gain
By successfully avoiding pain.
And if we summon up the will,
We have the capital and skill
To achieve most social goals.
Not pouring money into holes
But based on a solid business case
And working at a blistering pace.
This can be social enterprise
Or businesses of any size.

And to my mind the real key
For businesses is synergy.
Good projects can always be found
Where there is a common ground.
By this it should be understood
Both business good and social good
Should be enhanced side by side.
And we have found when this is tried
There is a constant feedback loop
Both society and the group
Do benefit in many ways.
Shared value serves as well as pays.
Your market strategy succeeds
As you eschew wants for needs.
And strategists will surely find
Their strategies get refined.
All stakeholders get excited
And employees are most delighted.
As development is accelerated
New customers are created.
And CEOs find it exciting
To soar above the tough trench fighting
And solve big problems most disdain
Because they seem such a pain.
But truth to tell, you take a bath
When you tread the beaten path.
But when you push where no one goes
Success then flows, heaven knows.
At this stage I really ought to
Salute Professor Michael Porter.
The brilliant idea he conceived

Was admired and well received.
And so when we could see
The light, we turned to FSG.
With confidence, now I can say,
They know how to show the way.
They worked with our entire team
And mined the rich and endless seam
Of talent as well as empathy
That in our group we can see.

And from the dross extracted gold
To build a program big and bold.
We called it Godrej, Good and Green.
And what a journey it has been.
If you permit me now to quote
A poem, that I then wrote,
You will then see what we mean
By our Godrej, Good and Green.

Godrej Good And Green

"For rapid growth of the nation
The big constraint is education
And so we chose to train a million
Good thing the number isn't billion.
Some think that we are aiming high
But setting sights at the sky
Can help us reach a lofty height.
And if we try with all our might
In ten years surely we'll succeed.
Right now we have to plant the seed.

31

And at the start we may be slow
But soon we'll be in fuller flow.
And if we teach the youth to earn,
Enabling them to quickly learn,
Then all of us will get to spend
The demographic dividend.
While growth is good and is our right
We should always keep in sight,
As billions seek the promised land
Enough resources aren't at hand.
What we deplete we must restore.
While this is hard I'm very sure
That if indeed we are wise

We'll first reduce, then neutralise
Our water use and C emission.
And that will serve as our green mission.
Green energy will play a role
In fact we have a separate goal.
A one third share, that we may need
To well surpass, to succeed
In Carbon emission elimination
As green energy, in my estimation,
Is already in a dead heat
And very soon will compete
With fossil fuel resources
As costs will rise from newer sources.
But in my mind our final pillar
Will prove to be the real killer.
Making products good and green
By most of us it's often seen

As striving for either or.
But there's a case to be made for
Producing products which are seen
As being both good and green.
These attributes will help to sell
And this will turn out very well
By helping businesses to grow
Much faster and ensure the flow
Of cash to spend on good and green.
And this is how it should be seen.
And in due course this little seed
If nurtured well will surely grow.
By 2020 we will show
That all three goals can be achieved
And once results are clearly seen
Then the Godrej Group will be perceived
As championing both Good and Green."

More poetry penned by Mr. Nadir Godrej can be viewed at
http://www.nadirgodrej.com/

DR. SUBASH CHANDRA GOEL

CHAIRMAN
ZEE ENTERTAINMENT
ESSEL GROUP

" *Observe the organisational attrition rates as that is a good bench-mark of a leader's effectiveness* **"**

-DR. SUBHASH CHANDRA GOEL

Retaining talent plays one of the crucial roles in creating and sustaining businesses of the future. A good and effective leader knows very well that putting the right person in the right role is key to organisational success.

Having built the 'A Team' judiciously and with deep behavioural insights, he tunes and aligns them to the corporate vision.

In this era where talented people are constantly on the lookout for 'greener pastures' the very fact that a leader can convince his key people to align themselves with his philosophy and stick with his team, defines to a large extent the leader's success.

A leader par excellence and an extraordinary innovator, Dr. Subhash Chandra of Zee Ventures has forayed into more than two dozen business verticals, **with nine of them being firsts in the country**.

A serial entrepreneur, he is Chairman of Zee Entertainment and the Essel Group (approx. US$ 4 billion), among the many others in his business empire.

Humble, and a great believer in karma, Dr. Chandra is a visionary.

He has almost single-handedly grown the Essel Group from scratch, making it among other things one of the largest speciality packaging businesses in the world.

His other areas of business diversification include the television and media industry, the 'wellness' industry, and many others.

CLARITY OF THOUGHT LEADS TO CLARITY OF VISION

When asked about this diversity, he confesses that the success is due to pure 'clarity of thought' and this clarity of thought is based on the fundamental understanding of how human beings in society have progressed. The achievements may be termed as visionary, but such words are the obvious result when a business is successful.

And success is itself dependent upon multiple factors.

He enumerates three such factors – **Knowledge, Experience and Talent**, which he stresses are all different from one another other, whereas the general tendency is to club all three together.

KNOWLEDGE AND EXPERIENCE

KNOWLEDGE can be acquired. Academically his involvement was limited, but his learnings from life's lessons go a long way in shaping his thought processes. Starting early in life and having a definite purpose, played an instrumental role in his creating an empire almost single-handedly.

EXPERIENCE comes with time, and it is transferable. A strong believer in mentoring and training, Dr. Chandra believes that the young can greatly benefit from the experience passed on by the seniors. The valuable lessons learnt through experience can easily and should be shared, thus benefiting the organisation as a whole.

TALENT IS THE KEY

TALENT is something that lies within the Individual – you either posses it or you don't. According to Mr. Chandra, in order to be a successful person in a particular area, one needs some kind of talent required for that area. He believes that talent to succeed in business is of three types:

- Thinking talent
- Relating talent
- Behavioural talent

Though seemingly different, one needs these sets of talent to be successful. Mr. Chandra says, **"Talent is nothing but a repeated pattern of behaviour.** To understand it one has to practice it. One needs too consistently meet people, talk to people, understand people – for it is through the medium of people that business gets conducted."

When interviewing people, Mr. Chandra looks beyond knowledge and experience. **He looks for talent.** He probes into the personal ambition of the candidate. He sees where the person is going, in what direction. His observation and analysis of the individual is purely through the behavioural lens. Though in life not all talented persons succeed, one needs to constantly strive towards success. This does not come through book knowledge alone. In fact Dr. Chandra he owes his own success to his guru, who is his grandfather; and to his own well-developed sense of personal intuition.

THE PRIMARY PARAMETER
OF ORGANISATIONAL HEALTH

With almost 50 companies under his direct control and an equal amount of CEOs he personally supervises, he successfully manages businesses across the world. Structured monthly reports keep him informed about the health of his various businesses.

Things need to be fine tuned occasionally and corrective measures have to be taken. One needs to see if the leadership throughout the organisation is effective and robust, and whether the leaders in charge of the various business units display strong leadership qualities.

Observe the attrition rates in the business – they will be a very reliable indicator of organisational health. Business health equates to people health. When people are happy, business results are better.

A LEADER NEEDS TO BE INTUITIVE AS WELL AS SCIENTIFIC IN HIS APPROACH

A good leader is not only a good performer, but one who can moti-vate others to perform.

He feels intuition also plays a role a vital role in a leader's success. This reveals the spiritually evolved side of his personality.

Dr. Chandra also lays great importance and stress upon the Human Resource Division.

His Human Resource department is constantly learning how to identify leaders with an intuitive style to their functioning as he feels these would be the ones to effectively lead the enterprise in these turbulent times.

KEEP POLITICS AWAY FROM BUSINESS

I n Dr. Chandra's style **there is no room for politics** – something which he firmly believes can be detrimental to the effective functioning of any organisation.

Leaders may have their favourites, but that is basic human nature, to nurture those whom you like and depend upon. It should not be done at the cost of elevating an unworthy individual to a level where he is incapable of delivering to expectations.

Looking towards the growth and progress of the organisation should be the singular motive while promoting people to take up higher levels of responsibility.

RESPONSIBILITY TOWARDS SOCIETY

Dr. Subash Chandra has **always believed in giving back to society**. Even before the phrase – Corporate Social Responsibility (CSR) – got its current elevated status.

Social Responsibility is in his blood. Personally he contributes 10% of his personal earnings to philanthropic activities. Though the government has mandated 2% of profits to CSR (2014), Essel had passed this resolution on the Board more than 10 years back. Thus giving back to society has been ingrained in the philosophy of the organization

CSR to him is social awareness which should be part of planet awareness and should be the theme for all **responsible organisations**. Being **part of society, you have to be responsible to the next generation.**

USE THE MEDIUM TO
DELIVER THE RIGHT MESSAGE

Today media, especially television, is part of touching people's lives on an everyday basis. Dr. Chandra has a core team in his office which has the responsibility of overseeing if **under the guise of popular television programming, are they providing audiences the right message or not?** Whether they are setting society on the correct path through their programming content?

He strongly believes that through entertainment, one can send strong messages to viewers and shape their thinking and mindset. That television as a medium can be an important tool for social change.

Therefore the content shown on television is important in creating a conscious and evolved society.

A LEADER IS ALWAYS VALUE DRIVEN

He also is of the firm opinion that businesses should not only take decisions keeping the profit motive in mind, but focus primarily on doing business in a manner which is conducive to societal well-being

An example and anecdote he quotes in his own book, about how he was offered an opportunity to be the agent or middleman on an international arms deal. The night through, he could not sleep, and the next day he declined the offer, forgoing the 2% commission that would have run into the millions. Why did he lose out on this opportunity? Simply because the transaction was unethical to his evolved way of thinking.

Dealing in guns meant being responsible for the loss of lives, and therefore he made up his mind that he would not conduct any business deal connected with the arms and ammunition sector. Money, he says, you can make from any other business. But **values are sacred and should never be compromised.**

CONTRBUTE TO EDUCATING
THE SOCIETY YOU ARE PART OF

S o as a corporation are you being socially responsible or not ? Dr. Chandra says that an organisation's responsibility towards society should not merely end with thoughtlessly contributing 2% of its profits as per the CSR Act,

Rather, each organisation and its leader should question themselves, **"Through every CSR oriented action we take, are we genuinely helping somebody who is in need in society**? Or are your actions hurting someone knowingly or unknowingly.

CSR is not just a mandatory Act to be followed as far as he is concerned. It is not simply about accruing tax benefits. It is a strong pillar of development for society. Among the possible range of CSR activities, he believes that focusing on education is among the most important. By educating the society at large, it is his way giving back to society. This, he believes will secure the future of the nation and its people.

WALK THE TALK

He is the **Founder of TALEEM** (Transnational Alternate Learning for Emancipation and Empowerment through Multimedia). **TALEEM provides access to quality education through distance and open learning**. Dr. Chandra personally appears on his channels and guides the next generation by lecturing and answering questions. This demonstrates his direct involvement with causes which are close to his heart, and sends across a strong message that he 'walks the talk.' This is an extremely important leadership trait which generates credibility and trust.

He is also the Chairman of **the Ekal Vidyalaya Foundation of India, a movement founded to eradicate illiteracy in rural and tribal India**. This Foundation provides free education to nearly 11 Lakh children across 40,000 villages in 21 states, through single-teacher schools.

LET THERE BE A HEALTHY RETURN ON INVESTMENT IN EVERY ACTIVITY YOU UNDERTAKE

H is main theme is that the money you spend on philanthropic activities, whatever be the amount, **should give a benefit to the society.** According to him, the benefit should be at least double the contribution. It **should create an impact**. And this is possible when the giving is done with thought and care.

Some NGOs and some companies just get involved with CSR as an image building exercise, and for them it is just another activity where all that is done is that the organisational Human Resource function issues a cheque to any social cause.

But this to him, is not CSR with a heart.

As far as Dr. Chandra is concerned, **one needs to get involved with the social project in your area of interest and expertise, and take the onus of creating the best platform in that area for the next generation to stand on their feet**.

This is where true value comes into CSR.

As mentioned, Dr. Chandra does a show on his channels Zee Business and Zee News, where he comes on screen and personally passes on his knowledge (which has been acquired through deep study and experience) to the youth of our nation. This is also a type of CSR, where personal time, energy and efforts of the leader are involved.

INDIA IS WHERE THE FUTURE LIES

Indian academia does not focus on and talk much about Indian companies that have broken the glass ceiling, that have been innovative and involved in pioneering activities.

But this is not due to any lack of initiative and innovativeness on part of the Indian firms, which have achieved success in difficult environments with limited resources.

Thus emerging as well as developed markets ought to take lessons from Indian corporate houses on many aspects of management and leadership where great heights have been attained.

BE HUMBLE – BE HELPFUL

Our start-ups are a great source of inspiration, and their stories need to be told. The entrepreneurs themselves, while on one hand constantly scaling new heights, have to remain rooted to the ground.

As a leader Dr. Chandra emphasises that one got to be humble about success and also encourage budding start-ups and support new ideas, and incubate entrepreneurs and help them across the rough tides they may face in the early days of their new venture.

This is one of the responsibilities that successful leaders need to shoulder ass their contribution to the next generation.

GREAT LEADERSHIP GETS
UNIVERSAL RECOGNITION

What few know is that Dr. Subhash Chandra was honoured with an International Emmy Directorate Award (2011). This is a highly coveted international award that recognises excellence in television programming produced outside of the United States.

Once you are globally recognised for your contribution towards your field, not only are you respected wherever you go, but more importantly your organisation and your brand is viewed more seriously by all stakeholders concerned.

Truly, Dr. Chandra has succeeded in placing Indian television programming as well as Indian industry on the global map.

" Business should always focus on giving back to the society at large "

-DR. SUBHASH CHANDRA GOEL

In the 21st century, where the gulf between the rich and the poor is constantly widening, businesses should evolve as part of their corporate strategy as to how they can give back and contribute to the have-nots in the society of which the businesses are themselves an integral part.

This should become part of leadership thought and should not be delegated to a department who looks at it just a 'Corporate Social Responsibility' activity to be done mechanically, simply to fulfil mandatory norms.

In this manner, true social-business partnership can evolve and this synergy awakens the eco-consciousness at large, also setting an example for others to follow.

MARTEIN PIETERS

CEO ————
VODAFONE INDIA

> **" A good leader should be impartial and fair in his judgements and leave personal bias aside when he takes professional decisions "**

-MARTEN PIETERS

One of the hallmarks of a great leader is not to get prejudiced due to personal likes and dislikes when it comes to taking corporate decisions.

Too often it is observed that egoism and personal whims and vendetta come into play when employees tend to genuinely disagree and speak up when they feel the need.

This approach proves detrimental to the organisation and many companies hit the dust when the leader is not balanced and impartial in his decision making.

align themselves with his philosophy and stick with his team, defines to a large extent the leader's success.

By qualification, Mr. Pieters holds a Dutch Law degree from Groningen University, The Netherlands and completed a Post-graduate course in Economics in 1979.

Prior to being the Managing Director and Chief Executive Officer of Vodafone India, Mr. Pieters served as the Chief Executive Officer of MSI, which became Celtel, from 2003 to its acquisition by MTC in early 2007. During his tenure there, Mr. Pieters was a prime mover in Celtel's becoming one of the leading pan-African telecommunications operators, serving some 20 million customers in 14 countries. Prior to that assignment, he worked at KPN where, since 2000, he served as a Member of the Executive Management Board of KPN Telecom with specific responsibility for KPN's Business Solutions Division. He served as an Executive Vice President of KPN International Operations, covering Central and Eastern Europe, Asia, and the United States. Since 1995, Mr. Pieters served as Vice President of International Operations responsible for KPN's affiliated companies, including EuroWeb, SPT and Pannon GSM.

Before starting his career in telecommunications, Mr. Pieters worked from 1979 to 1989 at Royal Smilde Foods as a Director of Finance and Strategic Planning and also served as its Chief Executive Officer in the Netherlands.

Among the many other roles Mr. Pieters has played include being Chairman of the Board of Cellular Operators Association of India since July 2014, a Director of Social Investor Foundation for Africa, and also holding seats on the Supervisory Boards of various operators including Cesky Telecom and Xantic.

56

CLARITY OF THOUGHT
AND INCISIVE ANALYSIS

We indeed learned much from the substantial time we were privileged to spend with Mr. Pieters, and we gained tremendously from the first-hand leadership insights he shared with us. These are based on rich experience he has acquired through his many assignments at senior levels in leading multinational organisations across the developed and developing world.

His clarity of thought and incisive analysis of every issue we spoke with him upon left us in no doubt as to why this man is highly sought after as a professional CEO by the best of the brands in the world today.

A synopsis of the leadership insights gleaned by us from our interactions with him follows, and will make delightful reading.

THE KEY TO SUCCESS
LIES IN UNDERSTANDING

According to Mr. Pieters, the first quality that a CEO ought to possess is the inclination and the ability to **understand his people**.

He has to be **forever listening**, and be **alert**, to changes occurring all around him – be they changes in the business environment, the moods of people he interacts with, tastes and preferences of customers, and every new move his competition makes.

BE FAIR – BE JUST –
BE A PROFESSIONAL

A CEO's background should understandably prepare him for the technical aspects of his job.

But primarily a CEO should also be **impartial and fair in his judgments and leave personal bias aside when he takes professional decisions** as the entire organisation and its myriad stakeholders depend on his thought process, understanding, and decision-making prowess.

WHAT MAKES A CEO A SUSTAINED SUCCESS?

In brief, Mr. Marten Pieters defines the qualities of a CEO as:

- **Good Listener**
- **Empathetic Individual**
- **Determined and Driven**
- **Multi-tasker**
- **Delegator**
- **Self-confident**
- **Apolitical**

The above are what Mr. Pieters feels are the qualities a CEO aspirant needs to focus on developing and strengthening. Further elaboration by Mr. Pieters on each one of them follows.

BE SILENT AND LISTEN

A **CEO should perpetually be in listening mode**, irrespective of whatever else he may be focused on at any moment in time.

Not only business-wise, but also listen to his people and all that they have to say.

He should not just operate in an authoritarian 'telling mode,' as a lot of practical and profitable ideas come from down-up.
This acquired and practiced ability to listen is good for the business and also boosts the employee morale.

EMPATHISE WITH YOUR PEOPLE –
PUT YOURSELF IN THEIR SHOES

A CEO should have the ability to mould people and make them better individuals and team-players. This is not merely with the objective of getting the people to do what he wants, but developing a congenial atmosphere and working environment is good for the company and ultimately makes the business profitable.

To demonstrate the strength of his personal relationship-building skills, Mr. Pieters talks of people whom he has had reason to 'fire,' but they are still in touch with him. This is because it is not a 'person' whom he has fired, but rather he has only 'fired' or let go of the individual's ability to do a specific job.

Mr. Pieters' strength lies in the fact that he never reflects negatively on any individual, even ones whom he has asked to leave. He empathises with them as individuals and It may just be that the company has moved on and so too, should the individual.

He urges and advises potential CEOs to fine-tune this quality of empathy and feeling for the other person, as he believes it is a key factor to CEO success.

FOCUS, DETERMINATION AND DRIVE

M r. Pieters strongly feels that a CEO should always be focused. He should have the determination and drive to push the agenda of the company forward.

He should not get confused with the multiple priorities that will be thrust upon him. He should listen to everyone and respect all views, yet be strong-willed and driven from within.

He should not be diverted from his identified goals by road-blocks that may come along the way. Road-blocks need to be acknowledged and addressed, but as soon as they are overcome, the CEO needs to get back on original track.

He should not be overwhelmed with negative thinking, but keep a positive attitude and constantly make intelligent efforts to move the organisation in a forward direction.

SELF-CONFIDENCE IS GOOD – ARROGANCE IS NOT GOOD

A CEO should have confidence in himself and in his ability to take appropriate decisions.

It is permissible to fail, but the CEO should never avoid taking a decision – he should always use his judgment and take a call when a decision needs to be taken. He must never procrastinate.

Even if he is the last man standing, he has to take intelligent decisions as his decisions are relevant and crucial to the smooth functioning of the business.

In fact, taking crucial organisational decisions is primarily what the CEO is there for.

And the CEO will be driven to take decisions when he has confidence in his own abilities, experience and expertise.

But Mr. Pieters correctly cautions, "**Self-confidence is not the same as arrogance.** Self-confidence comes from primarily knowing ones' own strengths and weaknesses, and from the years of experience of how things are best handled in any given situation."

CEOs AND POLITICS DON'T MIX

"Don't play politics; don't allow your people to play politics either,"
says Mr. Pieters.

Organisational politics is unhealthy and counter-productive to smooth functioning and customer focus.

Mr. Pieters provides an example of how he handles attempts by his subordinates to play politics: "If person A sends me a mail about person B with some negative comments about person B in it, I simply forward the mail to person B and thus let person A as well as others in the organisation know that playing politics at work is not acceptable. Sometimes, if I feel the situation between the two can be smoothened out through face-to-face communication, I bring the two parties together and help them resolve their differences. I don't involve myself in politics. **I understand that It is human nature – that sometimes some people just can't or don't get along well with each other. That's fine by me**. But the thing is to not let politics fester and develop in a corporate environment. Kill it early as soon as you identify it. That's in the best interests of all concerned."

He does add that people may not indulge in office politics with bad intent, but it is driven by the survival instinct prevalent in human beings – the fight or flight syndrome. This is present in every individual and should be addressed by the leader in an empathetic manner by taking time and effort and letting individuals know that their valid concerns will be addressed and not taken advantage of.

HANDLE CHANGE WITH GRACE

-On the vital subject of '**change**' he believes that a CEO should be sufficiently alert and adaptable to be able to see change and effectively meet it.

A systematic person by nature and by design, Mr. Pieters firmly believes in having proper systems in place, but at the same time being flexible enough to adapt to changes of any kind.

That is where the **self-confidence** and **listening** aspects he has previously spoken about come into play. **These qualities enable you to anticipate and welcome change with readiness.**

VIEWS ON INDIAN
BUSINESS ENVIRONMENT

Marten Pieters is of Dutch nationality and has worked internationally – He has dealt and worked with companies in Western and Eastern Europe, in the USA, in Africa and in Asia, and of course most intensively in his home country – the Netherlands. **Having had broad exposure to diverse regions, he believes emerging markets, though differing in culture, are similar to one another in ideology.**

In India, the socialistic bent of society, and the old license or permit system necessary to conduct business, has left the country with a basic distrust for private businesses and hence a limited private sector, compared to the size of the nation and its population. He believes that the idea that the government and public sector companies (PSUs) can be more productive and beneficial for the nation than private partnership is a concept that does not hold true today, and according to him it clearly didn't work too well earlier either.

It took the country 30-40 years to discover this and India is now gradually opening up. But he feels the old mind-set is strongly entrenched and still persists. Also he feels that due to the fact that politics in India often is driven by relatively elderly men, (as compared to the age of national leaders in the rest of the world), the old-fashioned mind-set weighs society down and this needs to change. The perception that authority is equal to age must change as in today's dynamic world and marketplace; age does not have much to do with progressive thinking.

THE RELATIONSHIP
BETWEEN FAMILY-RUN BUSINESSES
AND PROFESSIONAL MANAGEMENT

The initial impact of the private sector in India was negligible; it consisted mainly of family-owned companies and family-run businesses. Having himself worked in family-owned enterprises, Mr. Pieters understands the mindset of the management in most such firms.

Being employed in a family-run business is not a career choice for a professionally-minded individual that he would recommend as a first option. In most such organisations, it is the family which is foremost; and it is the family name which needs to be carried forward. That is almost always the priority.

This is where the term '**promoter**' is unique, feels Mr. Pieters. He has not come across this term anywhere else in the world. But as he says, you can understand the word 'promoter' once you understand the concept behind it. A promoter is a person (or a group of persons) who puts his own money at stake in an organisation, hires professional management to run it, yet retains control through majority shareholding.

MR. PIETERS' APPROACH AS A CEO – A LOT TO LEARN FOR ASPIRING LEADERS

He feels that India is just about opening up to professional management. Whether in Information Technology or in the pharmaceutical sector, the leaders at the top oversee the movement of the company. It is their **vision** that sets the pace at which the organisation grows and the direction in which it proceeds.

At **Vodafone** (where Mr. Pieters is the CEO), **people down-the-line are given the authority to take decisions with regard to their work area, and accountability and responsibility for their decisions and actions is linked with this authority**. This gives the employees freedom and a sense of importance, which in turn enables them to think like entrepreneurs and helps them develop a better and more focused approach towards their job.

Some employees take this opportunity and make the most of it – others are not comfortable with this approach towards work, where they have to think for themselves and accept responsibility for their decisions and actions. These are the people who may have to move out of the system.

A lot depends on the employee and his attitude towards work. If a person is willing to take calculated risks based on intelligent research and analysis of data and is willing to share responsibility, he or she does well in the system. Some people find it difficult to make decisions. **Some teams do not feel sufficiently empowered to take decisions, and that also depends a lot on the leader of the team and his approach and attitude.**

Which is why having a strong leader for every work-team is critical.

PUTTING THE CEO QUALITIES TO WORK – MARTEN PIETERS' STYLE

Initially when Mr. Pieters took over at Vodafone, people were not used to taking their own decisions as it had not been part of the work culture, and hesitated to think for themselves. People used to approach him for approval, and then when he encouraged them to take their own decisions and showed them how to best do so, the mind-shift gradually happened.

As Mr. Pieters says: "**You've got to let the team come to their own decisions, and that is very empowering**. And it is a learning process, because then they become good leaders. "

He stresses on and adds to what he has already said about the all-important leadership qualities of empathy and listening: "When you are **empathetic** and **listen with an open mind, you hear a lot more beyond what is said. You understand the person behind the speech**. You get interesting debates, and various inputs from various places. And you understand the **people dynamics, the team dynamics, the competitive dynamics** and **you see benefits**. This is the fundamental mind-shift that enables you to lead, and become a worthy leader."

CEOs SHOULD WELCOME UNCOMFORTABLE QUESTIONS AND PONDER THE ANSWERS

Interestingly, he says that he has noticed the following phenomenon widely prevalent in India: **"if you ask critical questions, you tend to get shunned and labelled as a trouble-maker."**

Many persons in leadership positions feel uncomfortable when they are asked critical questions.

But Mr. Pieters is of the opinion that as a leader, **you have got to listen to critical questionings.**

He appreciates the insightful inputs that persons who are labelled as 'critical' and 'trouble-makers' provide, because as he says: **"Whenever I have noticed people criticise me or my decisions, they have always done so with insight and thinking; it could be something that I have forgotten to consider before taking a decision, or something I had forgotten to question, or even it could be that I was not smart enough to think of them!"**

So he welcomes criticism from all quarters and advises leaders and CEOs to appreciate and reflect upon criticism and not outrightly reject the same when it comes their way.

71

STEP ONE TO SUCCESS IS ROLE CLARITY

He also emphasises the importance of a well-defined **organisational structure** and **role clarity.** Many people are frustrated in their jobs, because it has not been made clear to them what their jobs exactly entail, and are not clear about how their manager appraises them.

While on this subject, Mr. Pieters believes that the Human Resources function plays a vital role in bringing about **role clarity** and **role definition to individual job profiles within the organisation**.

Human Resource manuals, organisational structure charts, development plans, and the like, all make for good reading, **but putting them into practice is crucial**.

You need to consistently talk with people and listen to them and plan outcomes and finally assess the output. Once proper plans are made and careful assessments done, the leader along with the Human Resources team can identify and develop **clear career paths**, and that results into more business, more profits, more bonuses for everyone.

Role definitions and performance appraisals need to be strongly performance based.

But performance itself needs to be objectively assessed. And that can only be done get once role clarity is established.

At Vodafone they have invested a lot of time and energy into creating systems for defining role clarity and assessing performance. This he feels was a good investment, as he believes that is what created clear career paths and motivated ambitious key performers to identify their future with the organisation and thus work harder and smarter.

A win-win situation for all concerned.

PEOPLE ARE THE PRIORITY

Considering all these factors which drive organisational success, Mr. Pieters personally invests considerable time on what he terms '**people issues**'. He does not consider them as merely 'Human Resource issues,' but 'People issues.'

Sometimes the approach he adopts towards them keeps changing, **but the basis and the foundation of keeping human beings at the centre and as the focal point of all strategic and tactical initiatives is always firmly kept in place**.

The challenge is to identify what works for people and keep doing that once all the Human Resource manuals and Information Technology systems and other organisational processes have been established.

COMMUNICATE YOUR MESSAGE
CONSTANTLY TO YOUR PEOPLE

Mr. Pieters believes that the challenges of the modern corporate environment – cultural differences, age differences, rapid development of technological advances and the like, need to be focused upon and given due consideration by the leader, but the bigger question always remains as to how **to get the key organisational messages across to all employees in a consistent manner**.

The communication has to be constantly there, and it has to be right.

HEALTH AND SAFETY
OF THE PEOPLE SHOULD BE
A CEO's CONCERN

Another key area that the organisation under the stewardship of Mr. Pieters focuses on is that of **Health and Safety.**

He feels that India needs a lot of catching up to do when it comes to workplace safety and safety of the population in general. He observes that China with a greater population than India has a far better record of safety, and that large organisations in countries such as the UK and Germany have only one casualty every two years or so.

He laments the fact that we in India do not value safety of individuals as we should be doing.

At Vodafone, health and safety is the Number One priority, and it is an area focused on at every meeting, and also whenever Outdoor Management Development Plans are considered and drawn up.

SOCIAL RESPONSIBILITY IS NOT JUST ABOUT ISSUING A CHEQUE

A s for the area of Corporate Social Responsibility (CSR), he **doesn't think it should be made mandatory by the government; rather the philosophy of societal responsibility should come from within the organisation.**

But he adds that organisations themselves need to feel the urge to be socially responsible and it is good for organisations to demonstrate commitment to the society within which they operate.

As Mr. Pieters puts it: "**If you are part of society, you should be a responsible citizen.**"

While he feels that India has by far too many rules, some sort of ruling on CSR is necessary. The government does have a role to play, and CSR needs to be regulated.

An organisation could theoretically fulfil its obligation towards society by just giving one cheque to the Prime Minister's Relief Fund, but that is not the way he would choose to do it.

He feels that **involving your people to contribute their time and expertise in worthy causes is healthy for the organisation as well as benefits the society at large.**

CUSTOMISE YOUR ORGANISTION'S
CSR IN TUNE WITH YOUR EXPERTISE

As a leading player in the telecom sector, Vodafone does have a far greater role to play in society than organisations in many other industries and sectors. In India, he has seen the reach of the mobile industry into the most interior areas and how it has **contributed to rapidly developing the society**. Thus he believes that the role of the telecom sector is far greater than say that of the perfume industry.

CSR is part of Vodafone's social contribution. It cannot be just a token contribution to fulfil the mandatory requirement. Doing it with a heart ensures the organisation's acceptance in society. It sends across a clear message that 'We too, are a worthy part of this country.'

CSR is our contribution to the development of the nation. The part we would like to play in the success story of India.

At Vodafone, the CSR priorities and initiatives are extremely focused and are channelised towards the letter 'E.' They are:

- **Environment:** In every act of Vodafone where they physically interact with the outside world, there is a mandate to ensure that no aspect of the environment is harmed or hindered in any way.
To reduce the carbon footprint, Vodafone has installed superior technology to help curtail electricity consumption and conserve energy. Sustainability is part of the priorities.

- **Education:** The best way of getting people out of poverty and to create equal opportunity is by giving them education. The mobile technology can facilitate this also.

- **Empowerment:** The focus here is on women and the thrust of CSR in these areas is project based. Vodafone tries to use its mobile technology to support initiatives in the area of women empowerment.

Also, simple applications on mobile phones can make the lives of traders much more efficient. Getting relevant information on the phone helps farmers to take the right decisions on what steps to take or where to sell their products.

THE INDIAN CUSTOMER IS QUALITY CONSCIOUS – OFFER HIM/HER QUALITY AND YOUR BRAND WILL SUCCEED

Ultimately, he sums up his take on leadership by saying: **"You have to be able to connect. And take ownership."**

Lastly, but not the least, every organisation exists because there are customers.

A customer needs a brand to serve him.

The customer **builds** the brand.

People need value for the money they pay for goods and services and therefore a strong brand is built over time only when it can deliver satisfactory value to its customer base.

Mr. Pieters strongly feels that every customer is quality conscious, and Indian customers are especially quality conscious. He says that a brand is developed by consistently improving the quality it offers year after year.

He admits that **"You can't keep a customer happy all the time but it is vitally important for every leader and every brand to focus on execution and ensure the customer is consistently satisfied, if not delighted."**

And his parting advice: **"Ultimately, leadership is a matter of faith – in yourself, in your people and in your brand. Do well and succeed."**

> **Some teams do not feel sufficiently empowered to take decisions, and that also depends a lot on the leader of the team and his approach and attitude**

-MARTEN PIETERS

EMPOWERMENT right down to the lowest level of hierarchy in the organisation is crucial for survival today. The old system of 'top-down' approach does not work in an environment where speed is essential and information is available at one's finger-tips.

Leaders have to take into consideration the fact that the 'knowledge economy' has surfaced, which has changed the rules of the business game. The new-generation workforce does not like being ordered and instructed, but prefers to have the liberty to think independently and take decisions at least at their level.

Thus organisations and their leaders should evolve from within by bringing in essential reforms to ensure the transformation in their business performance towards the outside world.

AJAY PIRAMAL

CHAIRMAN
PIRAMAL GROUP

A leader, above all, should possess integrity

-AJAY PIRAMAL

'Walk the talk' – an old adage, but a timeless one.

Integrity is what brands a leader and is a quality which people look up to a leader to admire and emulate.

The human being is emotional in nature and a display of integrity strikes positively at the human heart.

Leaders have extracted great work from their team when they have led with true passion and integrity.

In today's age, where the organisational brand is looked at in sync with the image of its leadership, it becomes of paramount importance that organisations of the future should be led by individuals who are uncompromising on ethical functioning and integrity.

By qualification, Ajay Piramal has graduated in B.Sc. (Hons.), holds a Masters in Management Studies from Jamnalal Bajaj Institute of Management Studies, and has completed the Advanced Management Programme from Harvard Business School.

In 2010, Forbes estimated his net worth to be US $1.0 Billion, which puts him in the ranks of India's Top 50 richest people.

He leads the Piramal Group, a diversified conglomerate with a presence across 100 countries. Under his dynamic leadership, the Piramal Group has evolved from a textile-centric business to grow to a US$ 2 billion conglomerate with diversified business interests across the fields of pharmaceuticals, packaging, financial services and real estate.

He is also the Chairman of Pratham, the largest non-governmental organisation in the education sector in India, which reaches out to 33 million children through its "Read India" campaign.

Among the noted past positions that Ajay Piramal has held are:

- Member, Hon'ble Prime Minister's Task Force on Pharmaceuticals & Knowledge-Based Industries constituted by the Government of India

- Member, Hon'ble Prime Minister's Council for Trade & Industry

- Member, Board of Trade Constituted by the Ministry of Commerce

- Member, Central board of directors of State Bank of India – India's largest commercial bank and is included in the "Fortune 500" companies

Mr. Piramal has also been attending the Annual Meeting of World Economic Forum in Davos (Switzerland) by invitation over the last one decade. He was a Member of the World Economic Forum's Governors' Forum on Healthcare and has often addressed at the WEF on various topics.

Among the multiple awards he has received over the years, some ones of special note are:

- "CEO of the Year Award" by World Strategy Forum in 1999

- Ernst & Young's Entrepreneur of the Year (2004) in the Healthcare & Life Sciences category

- Awarded "Entrepreneur of the Year" Award of UK Trade & Investment Council (2006)

- "India Innovator of the Year 2008" Award by CNBC TV 18

Ajay Piramal has also been nominated for the Forbes Philanthropy Awards 2013 in the Outstanding Philanthropist category.

He has also co-authored '**Light has come to me**', a book about management lessons inspired from The Bhagwad Gita, published by the Times Group.

All in all, a multi-faceted personality, and one who future CEOs could learn a lot from.

INTEGRITY IS THE FOUNDATION
OF ALL SUSTAINABLE LEADERSHIP

"A leader, above all things, should possess integrity. **Integrity is that point where one's thoughts, words and actions are all seamlessly aligned.** As a leader, one needs people to believe in you, and with that belief, work for you. Without integrity in thought, word and deed, it is difficult for you to have anyone aligning with you to become a part of your larger vision"

Thus does **Ajay Piramal** express his views on the singular, most important leadership quality he has identified in his long and successful journey in the corporate world – **Integrity**.

Since we spoke to him at length on the fascinating subject of leadership, he revealed to us some of the most important qualities any leader needs to develop and how they merge with the leader's success as he takes his people and his organisation forward. Some of these qualities he enumerated follow.

THE ABILITY TO WORK ALONG WITH PEOPLE

This 'gel well' factor plays an important role in the making of a leader, as during his role as head of a department, a brand, an organisation or an institution, a leader will come across people from diverse backgrounds with diverse mind-sets, and he needs to be able to work with them without unnecessary hindrances arising from biases and prejudices.

This works best when the leader is a '**people person**.' Some leaders are naturals at this, but even if you are not, you should actively work towards interacting more with all types of people you meet and get to know them as individuals rather than as mere work-related contacts.

A LEADER NEEDS TO BE
COURAGEOUS AND FEARLESS

He should be able to take the decision to wisely move on 'that path less travelled,' and once he makes that choice, he should commit his resources to successfully walk that path.

He should be **bold and decisive**. He should be able and willing to take strategic business decisions – decisions that are tough; decisions that are off the beaten path, for this is the reason he is chosen to occupy the leadership chair.

HUMILITY –
THE HALLMARK OF A LEADER

Humility enables a leader to learn from others, to listen to others and use these insights obtained from listening to come to certain conclusions, as a result of which he, his people and the organisation he leads will be better off.

This is when he will get the best out of his people and they in turn will be willing to engage with him in realising his goals and in fulfilling his dreams and corporate vision.

LEADERS DEMONSTRATE AN OPTIMISTIC AND
ENTHUSIASTIC TEMPERAMENT

Exuberant energy needs to flow throughout the organisation if creativity is to be sparked and teamwork and productivity given importance.

There has to be an air of **positivity** surrounding the actions of a leader.

Looking at a glass half-full or half-empty is a matter of personal choice, but identifying it as half-full rather than half-empty is the way to leadership success.

HARD WORK AND SMART WORK
TOGETHER WORK WONDERS

A leader needs to work as hard as or even harder than the people he leads. With competition getting fiercer by the day, there is no alternative to hard work.

At the same time, in a technologically driven world, where customers are getting more demanding for new products and services by the day, hard work combined with smart work ensures success.

A leader has to have the quality of being able to work hard to achieve laid-down goals in record time (without compromising on quality), and also inculcate this habit in those he leads.

MOVE SENSIBLY WITH THE TIMES

A leader needs to have a flexible mindset and also has to be open to change.

A leader cannot have a strategy cast in stone, but should be willing to previously modify laid-down paths to take advantage of a changing environment. A leader needs to listen to and embrace the challenges of change.

He should constantly be fine-tuning his laid down strategy to keep it in sync with the evolving times.

LEADERSHIP HAS TO BE LEARNED – IT IS NOT INBORN

At the end of the day, wisely observes Mr. Ajay Piramal, people acquire leadership qualities through experience.

No one is born with these qualities; they have to be nurtured.

It is very much like studying a self-learning course, which could be appropriately titled '**The Art of Excelling in Leadership**,' and once a person has mastered the parameters needed for leadership success, he is ready to take on any leadership role.

STAY CONNECTED 'DOWN-THE-LINE'

A part from the leadership qualities already outlined, leaders and CEOs need to be well connected not only with the outside world but also with what is going on under their noses, within their own organisations.

Often leaders and CEOs are not aware about what is happening down-the-line as they are disconnected from their people.

Certain leaders and CEOs only give their ears and time to a small coterie of people around them, ignoring the majority of valuable inputs coming from the outer eco-sphere.

This should not happen, and if it does, it could turn out to be disastrous for the organisation.

DEVELOP A VISION BUT BE GROUNDED IN REALITY

Leaders also need to be in constant touch with the markets and the changing and varied tastes of their customers. They need to develop their vision and form insights to scientifically identify how the future for their industry would look like. To achieve this, the leader needs to be grounded in reality. Obtaining regular feedback and conducting critical analysis of business systems and proceedings should be part of a leader's regular regime.

Based on this feedback and inputs, the vision roadmap for the organisation needs to be set by the leader in collaboration with other key team-members. Once this is in place, the vision and the philosophy of the business should be repeatedly communicated and percolated through the organisation so that everyone at all levels is in sync with one another and all are pulling in the same direction.

FEEDBACK IS TRULY
THE BREAKFAST OF CHAMPIONS

Within the Piramal Group (Mr. Ajay Piramal explains), feedback is taken from various levels and from people at varying designations.

This is done through meetings, surveys and the like. At Piramal, they have developed some very structured forms of employee engagement surveys. Feedback is encouraged and is provided and received in the form of an open loop.

VIEW THE WAY THE WORLD IS CHANGING

How does he invest the limited time he has at his disposal?

Mr. Piramal says that though he does invests substantial quality time with his various Group CEOs, he invests most of his time on identifying latest happenings and observing the way the world is changing and shaping up and also studying the expansion of global markets and the direction these markets are taking.

This one activity ensures he is always abreast of the current trends, and this is so vital for a CEO today.

MR. PIRAMAL BELIEVES
IN 'MAKE IN INDIA'

What is his take on 'Make in India?'

Mr. Ajay Piramal is highly patriotic and intrinsically believes in the power of Indian industry. At a recent global economic summit, an economist spoke of India's economic role on the global front. He talked dismissively of Indian companies not being able to make their mark in the global arena. But that, according to Mr. Piramal, is not a fair comment. There are many Indian companies that are well respected in the global arena. And there are many Indians placed at very senior leadership positions in leading multinational companies around the world. Indian intellect and business capability are respected the world over.

As just one such example, Mr. Piramal quotes the name of the Tata Consultancy Services (TCS) as a very renowned and respected organisation of world-class standard. The market capitalisation of TCS alone can certainly make Indian industry proud.

Mr. Ajay Piramal too has done India proud with the strong and visionary leadership he has displayed to carry forward his business group. He is well known for identifying business potential and growth opportunities beyond the natural curve. From a traditional textile-centric family-owned business, the Piramal Group which he heads is now a staggering US $2 billion conglomerate, with diversified business interests across the varied fields of pharmaceuticals, packaging, glass, financial services and real estate.

The Piramal Group is also credited with bringing in India's first mall, thus being the impetus for the retail revolution in India. Software was the next big sector (after Retail), to put India on the global business map.

We asked him where the future lies for Indian industry. As per his sage estimation and analysis, the next big industries which appear geared to take the Indian business world by storm are the Internet-based companies and on-line application-based telecom services.

IN WHICH INDUSTRIES DOES THE FUTURE LIE

B ut an entrepreneur expecting to tap into the next big opportunity need not restrict his focus to these Internet-based businesses alone.

According to Mr. Piramal, opportunities exist everywhere. One just needs to have an open mind, grab these opportunities, and make the most of them. **India needs its entrepreneurs because wealth is generated when visionary business ideas are brought into action.**

It is the mind of the CEO that needs to constantly explore new ideas.

The young generation in India is a generation living on hope and has been born in the age of abundance. They are confident of their abilities and are open to experimenting and taking risks and moving onto new paths with maverick ideas. In the olden days, a person graduated and got a job, and stayed on till the age of retirement. One wanted a steady income and a secured life. That was the norm for those days. Now times have changed and it is the entrepreneurial spirit that makes people embrace the 'new.'

HOW TO OVERCOME THE
CHALLENGES OF LEADERSHIP

What according to him is the greatest challenge that leaders face today?

He feels the biggest challenge at the leadership position is the changing of mind-sets or the old way of doing things. There will always be people telling you that you need not bring about change and to carry on with the old and traditional path. This is because they do not want to move outside their comfort zone.

But the leader and the CEO has to display the courage to move forward on a new track and take up the challenge of seeking new horizons. **The leader has to be clairvoyant in his approach – he has to scientifically predict the future and then head his organisation in that direction.**

A leader needs to **actively seek opportunities and meet them head-on**. He needs to **engage people as equals**; if one looks down on subordinates, new and fresh ideas will not flow upwards. A leader needs to get people engaged, encourage them, allow them to make mistakes, learn from those mistakes and move on.

TIMING IS CRITICAL

As mentioned, Mr. Piramal has always been on the look-out for new opportunities to invest in and grow. When Pharmaceuticals looked like a good option to Mr. Piramal, that is where he pushed forward. There were the naysayers; people who advised him to not enter new areas where his organisation did not have a presence, but the opportunity seemed profitable in the long-run, and he embraced it. The rest is history.

Equally important as knowing which business areas to enter at what time, is knowing when to exit a business. This is also a leadership skill which plays an important role in the success of any business conglomerate, and this has made the Piramal Group a leading Indian conglomerate to reckon with.

SUCCEED OR FAIL —
YOU ALWAYS GAIN EXPERIENCE

Mr. Piramal observes that when one ventures into a new business area, one is never at a loss.

What results when you take a risk in a new business area is either either **success; but even if you 'fail,' you get an experience.**

Experience by itself is worth it, if one learns from and gains from that experience. Nothing is wasted.

HIRE PEOPLE WITH AN ENTREPRENEURIAL MINDSET

Mr. Piramal notices that people differ drastically in their temperament and their approach towards work and also in their areas of interest.

People come with their individual flavour of talent; a leader has got to see that talent, **nurture** that talent, and take the risk of investing in these people to get the fruit of their talents.

Some people who apply for a job with your organisation may possess an entrepreneurial trait; one needs to take note of such traits and hire such individuals, take them on-board your team, and with their help build a culture of innovation within the organisation.

ALIGN YOUR SOCIETAL GOALS
WITH YOUR BUSINESS CAPABILITIES

S peaking on the important subject of Corporate Social Responsibility, Mr. Ajay Piramal mentions that the Piramal Group was one of the earlier investors in CSR activities in the Indian context.

Pratham, which is the **largest non-governmental organisation in the education sector in India**, is a Piramal venture and reaches out to 33 million children through its "Read India" campaign. This commenced way before the mandatory government regulation of investing of 2% of profits in CSR activities was introduced.

According to Mr. Ajay Piramal, CSR is the need of the hour and the demand for it is infinite. Mr. Piramal followed his passion when it came to investing in CSR activities. To him, since he believes that education is the leverage to the future, the field of education is where he prioritised the CSR investments of the Piramal Group. He firmly feels that CSR should not be done by counting the possible returns to the organisation, but rather it should be seen as a business goal and aligned with the purpose of doing social good.

Social welfare should have results visible in the social domain, and not be indulged in merely for monetary benefits and reasons of publicity.

MR. PIRAMAL'S INVALUABLE ADVICE FOR BUDDING ENTREPRENEURS

We asked him if he could share some advice for India's entrepreneurial talent.

Mr. Ajay Piramal's message to budding entrepreneurs is to go ahead and take the risk. Opportunity is aplenty in India and growing by the day.

The advantage for modern-day entrepreneurs is that starting a business in earlier days needed a lot of capital; but **today it is the unique idea and the speed of execution of the idea in the shortest possible time which matters most**. Ideas and hard work move together towards success. This is a boundary-less world that is uniquely taking shape before us, and we need to take advantage of it.

One needs to be ready for success, and also be prepared for failure. One cannot be disappointed with failure. Remember, failure is never final. One has got to build success upon the foundation of failure and forge ahead. Act decisively and steadily.

Develop and use your support system.

Ask the right questions to the right people.

One will often get help from areas where one least thought one could get it if one acts with honesty and courage.

Ultimately, follow the route of excellence, quality and delivery – that is Mr. Ajay Piramal's *mantra* for leadership and entrepreneurial success.

> ## **A leader needs to actively seek opportunities and meet them head-on**
>
> -AJAY PIRAMAL

When change itself is changing and the business environment looks different, dicier and murkier day-by-day, a leader should develop deep insights to seek opportunities amongst the challenges.

His inner-eye should be awakened and he should be able to prepare his team to identify and embrace the opportunities that are constantly emerging in the new business economy.

Passive and complacent leaders, who rest on past laurels and glory, will certainly cause great harm to their organisations.

The key mantra today is to be active and alert to context.

ANU
AGA

> **It is the values of an organisation which decide the path the organisation will take as it matures over the years**
>
> -ANU AGA

VALUES get formulated once a strong philosophy is set in place by the founders of the business entity. These values need to be communicated across the organisation which will then give a specific flavour to the culture that sets in.

These values having been established, then determine the future course that the organisation will chart for itself. In this way, the leader through personal value-systems, leaves behind a lasting legacy.

Anu Aga is soft as cotton-wool, sweet as honey, and tough as steel. In short, she has all the requisite qualities a leader needs to possess to succeed in these challenging times.

Ms Aga is amply qualified to lead a business conglomerate, having graduated with a Bachelor's in Economics from St Xavier's College, Mumbai and securing a post-graduate degree in medical and psychiatric social work from the prestigious Tata Institute of Social Sciences (TISS). She was also selected for a Fulbright Scholarship and has studied in the United States.

Nominated to the Rajya Sabha in 2012, she is known as much for her social work and devotion to causes as she is for her remarkable business achievements.

In 2004, she retired as the chairperson of Thermax Ltd, handing over the role to her daughter Meher Pudumjee, who is an able successor. (Thermax is a Rs. 4,935 crore engineering solutions provider in the energy and environment sectors, present in 75 countries of the globe.)

In 2010, Anu Aga was awarded the *Padma Shri* for her work in the social sector, where she has been involved with promoting communal harmony and nurturing education for the underprivileged.

Recently, Anu Aga was ranked No. 79 on Forbes magazine's Richest Indians list with a net worth of $655 million.

She is also renowned for her adherence to transparency in corporate governance.

THE HARD ROAD TO LEADERSHIP

Thermax Ltd. (INDIA) is a company based in India, which has also made boilers, has four manufacturing centres, and operates in seventy five countries. It became known as Thermax Ltd in 1980. In 1987 it started making vapour absorption machines, in collaboration with Sanyo of Japan. It formed a joint venture in 1988 with American-based Babcock and Wilcox (who make boilers), to make steam generation units for heat recovery steam generators (HRSGs). In 1992 it formed its Combined Heat and Power Group.

On 15 February 1995 it became a public company on the Bombay Stock Exchange. In 2009, it signed a 51:49 joint venture with US firm SPX Corporation to provide equipment and services for the Indian power sector.

Thermax was set up by Anu's father Mr. A.S. Bhathena in 1966 as Wanson (India) to provide a range of engineering solutions. The company was renamed Thermax in 1980 after her father retired. Anu's husband, Rohinton, then headed Thermax till 1996, when he died of a massive stroke.

Anu Aga then took over the lead role at Thermax, and while she was still settling down in this critical role, she suffered a second personal tragedy - her 25-year-old son Kurush was killed in a road accident.

At this time, Thermax's growth also suffered a setback, with its share prices plummeting from Rs 400 to Rs 36, partially because of a market downturn.

It was around then that an anonymous letter from a shareholder to Anu Aga, accusing her of letting him down, forced her to take stock of the situation. Realisation struck her that as the largest shareholder of a public limited company, it was her responsibility to turn the company around even if she personally felt she wasn't cut out to be its chairperson.

111

She initiated a full-scale reform and turnaround of the organisation with the help of the Boston Consulting Group. In this manner, between February 1996, when she took over as chairperson of Thermax, and 2004, when she gracefully stepped down and handed over the top post to her daughter Meher, Ms Aga transformed Thermax into a global turnkey player in energy and environment projects.

THE VALUES OF THE ORGANISATION DERIVE FROM THE VALUE SYSTEM OF ITS FOUNDERS / LEADERS

The stated values of an organistion reflect the values of the founders/ leaders, and serve as the guiding light for an organisation whenever any decisions are to be made.

It is the values of an organisation which decide the path the organisation will take as it matures over the years.

And it is these very values which, if chosen with care, and communicated with personal example throughout the length and breadth of the organisation by the leaders on a regular basis, ensure sustained growth and success.

This has been the case with Thermax, and the reason is not far to see – the strong and eternal Values chosen by Anu Aga and her predecessors and successors at the helm of affairs at Thermax, an organisation which serves 75 countries of the world.

All organisations and their leaders can learn a lot from the values that Thermax holds dear.

It is indeed values which steer an organization onto the correct road, without which there is no direction.

What follows is a list of the values which drive Thermax on its path forward:

'RESPECT' IS AT FIRST POSITION

No organisation can survive or succeed without respecting others and their contributions, and also respecting their very existence. At thermax, the value of 'respect' extends, but is not limited to, the following entities:

- Respect for human lives and human dignity

- Respect for **WHAT** is right, and not **WHO** is right

- Respect for diversity – religion, caste, gender

- Respect for systems and processes

- Respect for performance, behaviour and discipline

THE NEXT CRUCIAL VALUE IS
'COMMITMENT'

M eeting a commitment made is what makes a brand and its leadership
credible and believable.

In a marketplace where 'trust' is a commodity which is in short supply, and
organisation which keeps to its commitments positively stands out as one
which all stakeholders would like to associate with.

At Thermax, the meaning of this value simplifies into the following:

- Deliver what is promised to all our stakeholders

- A commitment for excellence in all that we do

HONESTY AND INTEGRITY

These in fact form a USP or unique selling proposition for the best of leaders.

In recent years, we have witnessed so many leading global brands fall by the wayside for lack of practicing honesty and integrity in their business dealings.

Brands which have otherwise been technically sound and have excelled in their product or service offerings, have literally 'shut shop' because their leadership has let them down on these parameters.

At Thermax, the values of honesty and integrity find their roots in ensuring:

- Being true to ourselves in our personal and professional dealings and doing what is right at all times

- Nobody will exploit the company for personal gain or gratification

CONCERN FOR SOCIETY AND THE ENVIRONMENT

In the current era, which has seen heightened levels of awareness with regard to environmental degradation and societal welfare, this is a value which is integral to an organization being accepted and viewed favourably by the society within which it operates.

But Thermax does not view this as one of their core values because of reasons of publicity and a 'feel-good' factor, but because they actually believe in the same.

At Thermax, concern for society and environment specifically translates as:

- Encourage reuse, reduce and recycle, energy conservation

- A strong sense of giving back to society

- We must remember that business cannot survive in a society that fails

GREAT BLEND OF VALUES AND INNOVATIVE AND SUPERIOR PRODUCT BUILD A STRONG BRAND USP

What a specific and comprehensive set of values.

In other words, the 'Thermax Values' encompass **NO SHORT-CUTS** (Respect for systems and processes), an intrinsic belief in Corporate Social Responsibility, no partiality or bias (Respect for religious and cultural diversity), walking-the-talk (Being true to ourselves….), and literally all else that is necessary for a firm to be successful and respected in today's turbulent times.

And apart from needing to have clear values firmly in place, a corporate entity cannot sustain if it does not have an appealing product USP, which Thermax definitely has – being one of the few companies that can provide integrated offerings in the critical areas of energy and environment.

GREAT LEADERS ARE PERSONALLY INVOLVED IN CSR ACTIVITY

Thermax (as a corporate entity) and Anu Aga (as an individual), believe strongly in giving back to society as well, and when asked about her personal initiatives in the arena of Corporate Social Responsibility, Anu replies that she supports various NGOs / organisations / individuals through personal philanthropy for education for the underprivileged and encouraging initiatives in different parts of India for reaching out to the most marginalized children.

She also supports NGOs working for Human Rights and making elections free and fair.

Apart from these being her personal initiatives as these are causes close to her heart, Thermax as an organisation also has done more than its fair bit in its role as corporate citizen.

Thermax has chosen as its area of CSR work the improvement of education for underprivileged children and has also established the 'Thermax Foundation' to spearhead its CSR initiatives. Along with its NGO partner, 'Akanksha,' Thermax Foundation signed a 30 year MOU with Pune and Pimpri Chinchwad municipalities to run six schools.

And in addition to supporting the educational initiatives of Akanksha, Thermax also partners with Teach For India (TFI) to bring about a positive systemic change so that the quality of education improves for every child. TFI currently has 887 fellows working in India in 6 cities and impacts 30,248 students.

Anu humbly mentions that Thermax sets aside 3% of the company's net profits for CSR initiatives, **a sum which exceeds the mandate of the government in this regard.**

THINK BEYOND PROFIT

The CSR projects of Thermax have not been initiated simply because 'something needs to be done somewhere,' but rather they have been carefully chosen with a lot of thought.

Anu adds that "Our CSR programme comes from the conviction that corporates should think beyond profit and contribute to the well being of the society. In a country like India, which is marked by economic inequality and deprivation of large numbers of people, **we think that education can make all the difference to the lives of people**. We decided to focus on education of the less privileged to make change happen. Education can help people to come out of poverty."

A noble thought, backed up with resource allocation by Thermax.

Related to the subject of CSR is the area of 'Inclusive Growth;' a hot-topic in the country today. As a corporate leader, we asked Anu her opinion with regard to the same. Her response was characteristic of this societal-oriented leader: "The wealth and profit generated by productive activity should reach the millions of people now excluded from the development process. The State and civil society should work together to provide educational and livelihood opportunities, and a harmonious social atmosphere for all sections of people to lead gainful lives."

She goes on to add: "If the question is about socially conscious business, I would say that ultimately all business activities should be anchored in the concept of social well being. In that sense, there is no dichotomy between business prosperity and social development."

GREAT LEADERS ENVISION
THE FUTURE THOUGHTFULLY

Naturally, as an individual who has experienced so much and contributed so much to the nation, we were curious to know what vision she held for the 'India of the Future.'

Anu thought, then said, "A growing, prosperous country which wisely protects and makes use of its diverse and plural traditions, where people of all regions enjoy the benefits of education and health, where development happens in harmony with environment and where our leaders unite and not fragment people."

Words of wisdom which we wish those in positions of power would adopt as their guiding philosophy.

THE THREE MOST IMPORTANT
QUALITIES A CEO SHOULD DEVELOP –
ACCORDING TO ANU AGA

A nd in conclusion, we asked her the question that all readers would be most eager to hear the answer to: 'What are the three most important traits you think a CEO should have in this modern environment?'

Her response, which all leaders and aspiring leaders would do well to reflect upon:

1. The ability to 'read' the global business environment

2. Take good care of one's people

3. Align and integrate self and the organisation to the larger well-being of society

Thank you, Anu Aga, may more leaders like you grace the Indian soil in the years to come.

" Energy conservation should be 'top of mind' for a leader "

-ANU AGA

Environmental consciousness and energy-related issues should be of great concern for any leader, especially one who heads a corporate entity.

Energy resources need to be carefully moulded into the policy-making of an organisation, bringing awareness among the workforce.

By innovative thinking and waste-management, organisations today can increase their profit margins and become more competitive and viable.

DR. LALIT
KANODIA

CHAIRMAN
DATAMATICS

> **" *To be a leader, you have to be the best. Great leadership performance has to become a part of your DNA* "**
>
> -DR. LALIT KANODIA

Leaders should set their sights on excellence in every endeavour of theirs in the 'business game.'

An eye-for-detail and a spirit to relentlessly pursue the best business practices and standards of quality should be at the top of the agenda of a true leader.

Great patience should be displayed in inducting this spirit of excellence among the subordinates and the workforce, for it is only through excellence in product and service that the businesses of the future will survive in eras of extreme competition.

In the emerging markets of tomorrow, India can show the path through frugal engineering and native thinking, thereby

Dr. Kanodia has been a leader and innovator for more than half a century.

He graduated in B. Tech (Hons.) from IIT, Powai, Mumbai, and did his MBA and Ph.D. in Management from Massachusetts Institute of Technology, (MIT), USA.

He has also taught statistical decision theory at MIT. His journey in software started in 1965. He was retained by the Tatas to write a Project Report on starting the Tata Computer Centre, as TCS was then called.

He then returned to the USA, to MIT to complete his doctorate, and **then was invited back by the Tatas to start and head a newly formed company - Tata Consultancy Services**.

Dr. Kanodia was the first head and founder CEO of TCS (Tata Consultancy Services, a giant in its field today.)

Dr. Kanodia thus founded and pioneered the IT sector in India almost 50 years ago.

He is the founder of the Datamatics Group of Companies, where he heads all innovation, new product development and quality initiatives. His inspirational leadership has led Datamatics to be conferred with various awards over the years, including the 'Most Innovative Software Product Award,' the 'International Asia Pacific Quality Award' and also being ranked among the top 50 best managed outsourcing vendors by 'The Black Book of Outsourcing'.

He is an Executive Member of NASSCOM, the apex body of the IT-BPO industry in India.

He has served as the President of the Management Consultants Association of India, is an international consultant, and has held the post of consultant to Ford Motor Co., USA.

He won the distinguished Alumnus Award of IIT, Mumbai at their 25th Anniversary Celebration in 1983 for "Entrepreneurship" from the President of India.

128

REBUILD THE INDIAN SPIRIT
OF ENTREPRENEURSHIP

"One of the things that **India and Indians lost** in the last 200 years or so is **pride in ourselves and pride in our country**." Words of deep hurt and insightful observations coming from Dr. Lalit Kanodia, Founder of Datamatics Group of Companies.

India had its hey days many centuries ago. About 200 years ago, India had 23% of the world's GDP and 27% of the world's exports.
We seem to have lost confidence in ourselves today.

Besides IT, there is nothing significant emerging from this country that makes us swell with pride. We have also **lost our entrepreneurial spirit and enterprise**.

NEED TO RE-INVENT INDIA'S PAST
GLORY AS KNOWLEDGE LEADERS

India gave the world the calculus, the written script, the number system, zero and many more discoveries.

Ancient university complexes such as Nalanda and Takshila Universities had people coming from all over the world to learn there.
We knew the earth spun on its axis, we knew the earth revolved around the sun, we knew astronomy, the solar system, and gravity, centuries before they were discovered elsewhere.

But today, unless something is **acknowledged by the outside world, we in India don't value it**.

Protecting our IP and copyright is another issue altogether. Take the recent case of the patenting of Basmati rice where we had to fight to gain control f what has been ours for thousands of years.

HAVE FAITH AND BELIEF IN OUR INNOVATIVE ABILITIES

In America, you can invent something, build on it, develop it, customise it and sell it; there is a market for it.

In India there is **no such zest for funding new ideas**.

No one is ready to believe in you, till you start to make profit. Initial funding is scarce.

Investment needs to be a collaborative effort. It needs an initial push; not only by the private sector, or universities, but also by the government.

The **sense of trust is absent today**.

INDIANS ARE SECOND TO NONE
IN INFORMATION TECHNOLOGY

Companies worldwide today are **scared of the strong abilities of the Indian IT sector.**

We are the best and there is fear in the eyes of the competition.

Datamatics has been awarded quality certifications at the highest international level; viz. SEI CMM Level 5.

In fact more companies

FOCUS ON QUALITY
IN WHATEVER YOU DO

Again, according to Dr. Kanodia, while **marketing and branding are indeed crucial and very important, quality is equally important.**

Datamatics and the IT industry as a whole are on a journey of **quality.**

Datamatics has won awards on both quality and on Corporate Governance. This is a testimony to the stress they la on **world class performance and bettering world class standards.**

Dr. Kanodia believes that in order to be a leader, you have to be best. **Being the best has to become part of your culture.**

A leader has to aspire to be at the top. This means **he has to be the best and give his best.**

LEADERS CREATE CONDUCIVE ENVIRONMENTS FOR TRAINING TO BEAR GOOD FRUIT

A factor that bodes well for India is its level of higher education.

Generally **education and economic development have a direct correlation, but India is an exception**.

According to Dr. Kanodia, we can leverage this current exception to beat the world.

We also need to bring in a practical approach, together with our education. The practical skills that are required to harness the productive aspects of a subject should take place together with higher academic education.

In India, we have the talent and intellect. We are on par with people across the world when it comes to intelligence and talent.

It is unfortunate that our environment is not very conducive, and this is where the focus needs to lie.

At least within your own organisations, make the environment and conditions conducive to extracting the best from your people's talent and intellect. This is a vital part of the role of a leader.

DON'T FOCUS ON LOW PROCE ALONE – MAKE THE MOST OF YOUR COMPETITIVE ADVANTAGE

Every country leverages the unique selling points (USP) of the products that it specialises in manufacturing.

Pricing should not be the only differentiating factor though, in a competitive world price does matter.

We nevertheless have to create 'Brand India.'

Electronics has the 'Made in Japan' tag a success.

Now the focus has shifted to 'Made in China'. It is estimated that 25% of the world's manufactured output comes from China.

We need to leverage our inherent strengths to secure global competitive advantage.

THE OPPORTUNITY LIES IN
THE MANUFACTURING SECTOR

The economies of most countries developed from the route of agriculture, to manufacturing, to services.

Manufacturing comprises only 15% of India's GDP.

In China the corresponding figure is 45%.

India is losing out in catering to the huge global and domestic demand in the market for manufactured goods. We need to do the leapfrog in the 'manufacturing race.'

Today, not many entrepreneurs want to get into a manufacturing business because of the non-conducive conditions prevailing in the form of regulations, laws and policies. A complete mind-set change needs to take place if India wants to be part of the great manufacturing nations in the world.

GO FOR APPRENTICESHIP AND BUILD
A SOLID CAREER FOUNDATION

We need to provide vocational, apprenticeship and **skill training so that local industries and brands get created.**

The apprenticeship route and vocational training is what is strongly advocated by Dr. Kanodia.

The same has worked in Germany, and Japan.

In India, apprenticeship is unfortunately viewed as a low-end start to a career. Nothing could be further from the truth.

In fact, the **apprenticeship route is very valuable**. It is a **learning process**.

Just a plain graduate degree, from even the best university, or the best college is not adequate to get jobs. Experience and practical hands-on training **is needed and that's where apprenticeship plays a key role.**

KEEP AN EYE OPEN FOR LEADERSHIP TALENT – FUTURE LEADERS CAN COME FROM ANY BACKGROUND AND BE OF ANY AGE

The average age of the CEO is getting younger. It is the sign of our modern times.

Age no longer is a measure of seniority. This is because of the **velocity of change**.

Younger CEOs know the changing times better.

While age has experience on its side, younger CEOs are more **adept to technological changes and have the capacity to take risks**.

CEOs today come from diverse backgrounds; it is their mind-set and **talent** that makes them what they are, and enables their companies to grow.

Identifyingleadershiptalentisaprocess.Sometimesyou'grow'CEOsfrom the ranks f your organisation, sometimes by seeking talent from the outside.

Spotting talent is an art. Unfortunately, many managers try to suppress these talents they spot in their subordinates, as they see them as potential threats.

THE THREE MOST IMPORTANT TRAITS
OF A CEO – ACCORDING TO DR. KANODIA

When asked about the top three qualities a CEO needs to have in to-day's times, Dr. Kanodia gave extremely insightful answers, which would be of great help for our readers.

According to Dr. Kanodia, the important traits present and well developed in a CEO should be:

- **Ability to take tough decisions as situations demand**

- **Ability to identify, hire and nurture talent**

- **Ability to enter and exit businesses and markets as per business need**

ULTIMATELY THE SUCCESS OF THE BRAND IS THE RESPONSIBILITY OF THE CEO

D r. Kanodia gives examples of the Tata Group and of their exceptional ability to develop great brands, e.g. Titan and Tanishq, which have captured the interest and imagination of the old and the young alike. He cites these brands as excellent role models for entrepreneurs who may wish to grow their own brands from scratch. Of course it is the entire team at Titan and Tanishq which should take credit for their brand's success, but it is the CEO who bears the maximum burden on his shoulders.

He also says that it is the CEO who can make or break the success of an organisation or a brand. Citing an example of the brand 'Ultra-Tech Cement' was part of the L&T group, but was not doing well. Once the brand was taken over by the Aditya Birla group, it became a huge money spinner and a great brand.

STUDY AND TAKE ADVANTAGE
OF BUSINESS CYCLES

Business also has to be done in the way that it is immune to market cycles.

Most industries go through business cycles. Presently the service sector in India is 'on the high.' It is growing and needs to grow and will grow even further.

A business in the service sector needs multiple portfolios to thrive and expand.

The way to meet that challenge is diversification and growth – lateral, horizontal and tangential.

CSR SHOULD IDEALLY COME
FROM WITHIN, NOT ENFORCED

S witching to the subject of Corporate Social Responsibility (CSR), Dr. Kanodia feels that it is a good initiative by the government to have made CSR mandatory, but the **spirit of social welfare has to come from within**; be it from within an individual or a corporate.

CSR should not merely be a tax deduction issue.

Enforcement of CSR is not a bad thought, but the wellbeing of society should ideally be a part of inner consciousness. **The Tatas and the Birlas did it years back without any government pressure**.

Dr. Kanodia believes that focusing on social welfare, healthcare, education, should be the work of the government, not private business. Private organisations should lead businesses, not social welfare, which is secondary for business objectives.

But adopting a CSR cause can espouse business interests too. It is possible to work within your core area of expertise and contribute to society. **Use your business systems and processes to help others wherever possible**.

THE BASIC HUMAN
DESIRE IS TO DO GOOD

The Datamatics group has followed CSR in two core areas according to Dr. Kanodia viz.;

- Datamatics works with the physically disabled, who operate from their home, online

- **Datamatics has adopted the environment.** It has helped in the green movement, by enabling tree plantation and forestation. This benefits all. And all this was done more than 20 years back. It was a self-driven thought, a **focus on enablement**

So in effect, according to Dr. Kanodia, a CEO's vision merges and blends with CSR activities when he starts **feeling for the planet as a whole.** Doing **good for humanity.**

Dr. Kanodia reiterates, '**all of us want to do good**'. But here again, there are two factors involved. **The ability to do good** stems from both **whether a person can afford it**, and whether he has an **opportunity to do it.**

The basic human desire is goodness and is not evil. **If we can mesh that goodness with philanthropy it helps society, and that is what the philosophy of true 'win-win' is all about.**

" We need vocational guidance, apprenticeship opportunities and skill-based training so that local industries and brands get created and firmly entrenched "

-Dr. Lalit Kanodia

India is an extremely diverse market where 'one-size' simply cannot fit all. Having understood this, it is extremely important to create products and services which befit a particular region and customer mindset. By establishing localised products and brands, one can truly give a boost to the economy and at the same time generate wealth and employment at a local level.

Having a lopsided view by giving extra focus to management education and not sufficient attention to vocational skills and training, we have 'missed the quality bus.'

But it is never too late to re-look our priorities and invest in our diverse local talent, thereby enhancing the involvement of the youth and creating a stable economy and society.

MARTIN
KRIEGNER

CEO
LAFARGE INDIA

> **" You've got to be humble and you've got to be willing to listen and learn "**
>
> -MARTIN KRIEGNER

One of the most noble elements of human nature is humility. Humility brings about a natural human connect at the emotional level.

To further enhance and entrench the obvious benefits of this factor, leaders need to **LISTEN** to their workforce and their customers on an ongoing basis. Such listening then gets converted into the **LEARNING** paradigm.

When all this happens, brands begin to evolve, employees are happier and motivated, and customer service begins to shine and sparkle.

M r. Martin Kriegner is the Chief Executive Officer at Lafarge India Private Limited.

He has built his career with this organisation, serving Lafarge in various capacities in countries all over the world.

Lafarge is a French company specialising in three major products: cement, construction aggregates, and concrete.

The company is a world leader in building materials.

Martin Kriegner graduated from Vienna University Law Centre (Doctorate) and from the University of Economics in Vienna

HUMILITY IS ESSENTIAL IN YOUR LEADERSHIP JOURNEY

"You've got to be humble and you've got to be willing to listen and to learn" – These wise words by Mr. Martin Kriegner, Country CEO of Lafarge India, are a resounding philosophy that one should follow on the path to success, both as an individual and more importantly, as a corporate entity.

An Austrian national who has lived and worked in India on and off for almost fourteen years, Mr. Kriegner has built his philosophy of listening and learning by trying to understand and grasp more about the country, its markets and its people by **keeping a firm ear to the ground**. It is his innate humility that has helped him in understanding the 'ethos' that is India.

It is also his willingness to listen and to learn, which has led Lafarge India to involve themselves more deeply into the lives of and demonstrate genuine concern for the welfare and development of people, and also the villages surrounding their plants throughout the country.

LEARNING AND LISTENING

According to Mr. Kriegner, being fundamentally humble translates into the development of two valuable personal characteristics, which make for excellent leadership:

The First of these is LEARNING – You cannot rest on your laurels. Discover new facts and facets; to develop your knowledge base, to understand and assimilate local conditions, markets, customers and environment, which in turn helps the leader take the organisation towards business growth and leads to the path of better profitability.

The Second is LISTENING – While listening, you learn a lot. In fact it is correctly observed that one never learns anything while speaking; one learns only while listening. A leader needs to listen to his people, to his customers, to all stakeholders. Once you have listened well, you can translate what you have already learned from your broad and global experience, add to it the inputs obtained from the local experience, and define the local business model, which will help your business gain momentum.

MR. KRIEGNER'S FORMULA
FOR SUSTAINED LEADERSHIP SUCCESS

So Mr. Kriegner's recipe for leadership success is simple and highly effective, and can be displayed in the form of a powerful formula:

Fundamental Humility = Learning + Listening = Growth + Customer Satisfaction + Profitability

INNOVATIVE SOLUTIONS
ARE THE NEED OF THE HOUR

Coming as he does from the field of construction and infrastructure development, Dr. Kriegner's views on what constitutes leadership have a lot to do with these vital sectors. These sectors are especially important for a country like India, which is seeing rapid growth and flux in its building and construction sectors.

Lafarge is a world leader and solutions provider in building materials, and a major player in cement, aggregates and concrete businesses.

The company aspires to building better cities around the world, through its innovative solutions by providing them with more [and where required, affordable] housing, and making them more compact, more durable, more beautiful, and better connected. In India, Lafarge is present in over 40 cities where they offer construction solutions for residential and commercial buildings, metros, roads and related areas.

HEALTHY WORK-LIFE BALANCE
LEADS TO WIN-WIN FOR ALL

But what matters most to Lafarge is enabling the lives of citizens in terms of ensuring a happy and healthy environment.

This is what Lafarge does best – **builds better cities through developing a clean, more liveable and green environment and by greater accessibility between cities.** Interacting with people, engaging them on the cultural and social side, decreasing commuting stress are key factors in healthy living.

Providing a balance between work, family life, private life, social interaction, as well as an element of spirituality are key essentials to generating a feel-good factor.

In fact '**Happiness in the City**' was a survey initiated globally by Lafarge and its values have been inculcated across cities throughout the world. The survey is in keeping with Lafarge's ambition, which is to contribute towards building better cities globally.

SMART CITIES –
NEED OF THE HOUR

Mr. Kriegner propounds that infrastructure and construction companies should be involved in town and city planning right from the design stage, infusing intelligent technology to make the city a better place to live.

He also believes that focusing on aesthetics as well as functionality in design help a city become more beautiful and this adds to the citizens' quality of life.

Innovative use of decorative concretes and other materials make for beautiful sights. Beautifully designed and finished construction makes residents want to maintain the city. This adds to cleanliness and hygiene, and safety and convenience are its result.

This also enables the feel-good spirit. It adds to the investment of corporate houses in offices, and boosts the tourism factor as well, and hence the city prospers.

All this is in line with Prime Minister Narendra Modi's visionary thinking for smart and beautiful cities.

GLOBAL EXPERIENCE ENRICHES
A LEADER'S PERFORMANCE

Lafarge, being in the construction business, does not function in isolation but works in close coordination with people to improve lives.

There is a lot of potential for introducing technology into this sector; not only European and North American cities, but even cities in Asia such as Dubai, Singapore and Hong Kong have shown the way.

And that's where the rich global experience of a leader who has had international exposure helps.

The market is local, the needs of the customer are local, the climate is local, construction is done according to local conditions, using local raw materials; but the **expertise and experience of the leader being global helps benchmark the guidance and direction he provides against the best in the world**. This sage advice applies not only to leaders in the construction industry, but in all other industries as well.

UNDERSTAND YOUR CUSTOMERS AND FULFIL THEIR LARGE AND SMALL EXPECTATIONS

While understanding the customer in the construction business (as in any other business), local tradition, heritage and custom definitely cannot and should not be ignored.

Added to this should be a deeper **understanding** of how to **speed up the pace of construction without compromising on safety standards, adopting methods of construction which cause the least noise, pollution and environmental degradation in any manner, understanding the needs of the ultimate home user and owner in terms of heat, air conditioning, cross ventilation, comfort; in general to improve the final quality of construction.**

Solutions have to be found within the local constraints and conditions to succeed in the local marketplace.

SOCIETY SHOULD BE A BETTER PLACE FOR HAVING YOUR PRESENCE IN IT

Aligned with the concept of better cities is the philosophy of having better villages, **especially in a country such as India.**

By encouraging the various Corporate Social Activities undertaken by the company, Mr. Kriegner ensures that Lafarge constructively supports the villages and their inhabitants located around their cement plants in multiple, practical ways.

Lafarge is a firm believer in sustainable development; its commitment to this cause dates back to 1977. '**Sustainability Ambitions 2020**' is a long-term, comprehensive programme created by Lafarge, which encompasses all dimensions of sustainable development; namely - social, economic and environmental. It is the organisation's roadmap to make a net positive contribution to society and nature. Lafarge's sustainability ambitions are organised around three main pillars with nine major ambitions. The three main pillars are:

1. Building communities
2. Building sustainably
3. Building the circular economy

FOCUS ON ALL STAKEHOLDERS
AND THEIR NEEDS

These are some of the initiatives undertaken by Lafarge in India, which are in line with its global Sustainability Ambitions 2020:

- Water Management
- Climate Assist
- Education

Although the cement factories are not major users of water themselves, Lafarge enables villages within a certain radius of their plants to effectively source and manage water by building storage facilities for water conservation; ensuring proper irrigation and healthy flow of water; and enabling the management and harvesting of water in the dry months leading up to the seasonal monsoons. This ensures provision of safe and clean water to the surrounding areas, and helps support the water table; thus leading to better management of the environment.

When it comes to Climate Assist, Lafarge focuses on two key levers for reducing the CO_2 output. One of them is by ensuring the usage of Blended Cement; where Fly Ash is used in the cement making process; thus leading to improvement in the quality of cement itself, and also ensuring reduction of emissions. This benefits not only the consumer and helps build growth for the company; but the environment is the true beneficiary.

BE A THOUGHTFUL LEADER –
IN ALL POSSIBLE WAYS

L afarge prefers the use of Alternative Fuel, wherever and as much as possible, compared to depending on traditional sources, such as coal and other fossil fuels. In some of their plants, up to 10% of the fuel used is alternate fuel (which is a considerable amount in this industry) – these are waste oils and trade rejects, among other things.

This also helps the environment as it does not clog up landfills. This is a win-win situation – it makes good business sense as it assists productivity, and is also good for the environment.

Lafarge also assists villages in developing the next generation of productive individuals. It takes care of developing minor infrastructure towards schools, and also provides inputs and assistance towards education and skill development.

Some of the initiatives Lafarge has undertaken are linked to the vital element of employability; for example, contributing towards skill development leading to career and entrepreneurship opportunities, conducting masonry and carpentry training, and so on.

IF A LEADER WANTS TO IMPROVE THE ORGANISATION ON ANY PARAMETER, HE SHOULD MAKE IT A POINT OF FOCAL ATTENTION

Health and safety is the guiding principle of all Lafarge employees, and is the first ambition under its 'Sustainability Ambitions 2020' programme. This principle is geared towards ensuring safety in all walks of life and in all sections of society – road safety, work safety, etc.

Apart from workplace safety, the importance of safety is also inculcated in schools in the nearby community by Lafarge employees; and by passing on this important and potentially life-saving message to the children, the parents are influenced as well. Drivers are taught road safety through '**Defensive Driving**' training. Their road safety record is monitored and a 'no-untoward-incidents' status is rewarded by Lafarge; thereby encouraging people to practice safety and convert it into a habit through positive motivation.

Lafarge India, under the leadership of Mr. Kriegner, has cultivated the human approach and personal touch towards safety. There is strict monitoring and enforcing of safety polices in the workplace, since an injury or fatality causes havoc to the family.

Lafarge plants have a 'Lost Time Incident Frequency Rate' of a mere 0.08; where anything below 1% is considered world class. So their safety policies are already bearing fruit, ensuring that Lafarge is already ahead of industry averages on this important parameter.

This also demonstrates that any workplace parameter which is given importance and focused attention by the leader can be improved upon.

SPEAKING AND LISTENING
GO HAND-IN-HAND

Positive results emanate from management focus and people involve-ment. Unless management commitment and employee engagement are driven towards improving the safety issue (or any other issue which the leadership considers important), progress does not happen. Since Lafarge has focused on the parameter of safety, it is safety initiatives which are given maximum importance and fostered down the line.

But make no mistake, the initiative may be driven from the top, but **the way forward is a two-way approach – the management speaks as well as listens; and the people down the line, too, speak as well as listen; and ideas and initiatives are welcomed, or rather, encouraged, from all quarters. This is the way any leadership initiative succeeds.**

MEASURE THE RESULTS
OF YOUR ACTIONS

A lesson for all aspiring leaders to inculcate – the human way and the Lafarge way are in perfect synchronicity; and this is a primary driver of the success story of Lafarge in its business endeavours as well.

Mr. Kriegner says it is important and necessary that the CEO mindset and the CSR mindset are in tandem, so that social business and social awareness are part of the business model. This leads to a sustainable model; a win-win situation. Being a practical leader, heading a for-profit corporate entity, Mr. Kriegner rightly believes that CSR should not be a mere cost factor, but it should be designed intelligently in ways that benefit the company commercially too; not just for the feel-good factor.

Leaders need to measure the impact of their initiatives and their decisions – this is a valuable lesson that Mr. Kriegner provides to all aspiring CEOs. In this regard, he reiterates that measurement of CSR, its impact and its resultant benefits should be conducted on a regular basis.

Lafarge has devised an effective mode in this regard which others could follow. First, they identify the areas of need where CSR can lead to the maximum win-win. Then the initiatives are designed, resources are committed, the process is implemented, and then the progress is monitored and quantified. Only after seeing the benefits accruing from the initiatives can one know whether and how the chosen CSR initiatives have helped make a difference. **This monitoring and quantification also enables modifications or adjustments needed for better productivity and impact.**

YOUR PEOPLE ARE TRULY YOUR GREATEST ASSETS

A ll the above are possible because (and this should be a learning for any aspiring leader), Lafarge and its CEO genuinely believe in people.

A collaborative approach towards management is preferred and followed. The corporate vision is jointly created, taking into consideration views from all angles; conceptualised in a focused and structured manner; and then shared down the line.

It is the people across the organisation who convert this vision into reality.

This is all part of the **'listening philosophy'** passionately advocated by Mr. Kriegner. **Automatically adopting and implementing what has worked in other countries with different cultures may not be feasible in India; so a listening approach is critical.**

CRUCIAL LEARNING FOR LEADERS

The entire management team needs to be involved for crucial strategic tasks, and then given the resources and autonomy. That is when the leader can be assured that any task will be properly carried out.

The leader needs to be the driver of **commitment**; which Mr. Kriegner rightly defines as the **relationship between delegation and autonomy**.

A progressive leader needs to give people room to come up with their own suggestions and ideas, listen to all of them, and then implement the feasible ones.

Timely feedback is another necessary tool for a leader to ensure organisational success, according to Mr. Kriegner.

A leader constantly needs to assess and gauge his team's performance, functioning, and output; and see how much he himself is contributing to the team's performance.

This is an acid-test which a leader needs to perform frequently to check if his personal leadership matrices are on track.

A LEADER DEVELOPS EXPERTISE AND CONFIDENCE AMONG HIS SUBORDINATES SO THEY CAN FUNCTION INDEPENDENTLY

Ironically, the more a leader needs to get involved in contributing to a particular team's performance, it indicates that the team is not strong enough, or not developed enough, to achieve success on its own steam.

Leaders should not be hand-holding teams for an eternity; but should develop them in a way where they become independent decision-makers.

If a leader observes that a team is unable to perform without his constant advice and intervention, the team needs to be trained in areas which they need to build up on; provided motivation and encouragement to develop their self-confidence; and also provide whatever reasonable resources appear necessary to allow them to bloom to their full potential.

165

LEADERS NEED TO BE A KEY PART OF THE HUMAN RESOURCE FUNCTION

Thus, taking off from this, Mr. Kriegner feels Human Resources is a critical part of the CEO's function; and this function should be given substantial time and energy from his busy schedule.

Human Resource strategy and planning should be aligned with the overall business objectives and business direction.

Acute attention paid to the recruitment and selection of people, especially key decision-making profiles, is vital.

The right person in the right job can often mean the difference between organisational failure and success.
Talent is available.

Talent should be effectively tapped.

This is the key.

Mr. Kriegner personally and actively involves himself in the recruitment process of key positions.

INVEST SUBSTANTIALLY IN
TRAINING AND DEVELOPMENT

O nce hired, the development of people is not only in line with the business goals and objectives; but it also commences in the crucial areas of soft skills, and should be an on-going activity.

Individual Development Plan (IDP) is one aspect of people development, which includes functional, technical, and behavioural training and development.

Mentoring schemes are another mode of people development.

Training and development is such an important function that Mr. Kriegner believes in employing all available resources at his command; both internal as well as external, to enhance the potential of all employees.

Mr. Kriegner says: **"You've got to develop people up and down the hierarchy**. A leader needs to understand diverse mindsets and experiences of people on his team, and ensure they work together."

'MAKE IN INDIA' CAN
SOON BECOME REALITY

A ll this is not mere wishful thinking but is very much in line with Prime Minister Narendra Modi's '**Make in India**' dream project.

India has the necessary resources, has tremendous potential for becoming a global manufacturing hub because of its talent pool, its people, the level of education prevalent, its natural resources, its potential for growth. Lafarge aims to support these manufacturing initiatives commenced by the government to make the vision a success.

'Make in India' can become a reality.

Mr. Kriegner believes India has the capabilities to make the entire process of cement and concrete production self-sufficient; independent of any imports. **As an example, he mentions the automotive industry in India, which not so long ago consisted only of importing vehicles; now not only manufactures them, but designs and exports them as well.**

FOCUS ON PROVIDING AND TAKING UP APPRENTICESHIP – GERMANY AND AUSTRIA HAVE SUCCEEDED INDUSTRIALLY DUE TO THIS

Thus he advises the coming generation not to be averse to dirtying their hands and getting into the manufacturing sector, for that is where the foreseeable future lies.

Education and progress are two sides of the same coin. A thrust on providing apprenticeship opportunities and youngsters accepting them with open arms, will help in adding to the skilled workforce and ensure career security.

Mr. Kriegner provides the example of his native Austria and neighbouring Germany; where the concept of apprenticeship in manufacturing industries commenced initially as a government initiative. Private enterprise quickly saw its benefits; and now the thrust of apprenticeship in these countries is spearheaded by the private sector. **This fact alone (the thrust on apprenticeship) has been hugely responsible for development of industry,** heightened levels of productivity, and enhanced levels of quality in these countries.

Organisations in India, too, which can visualise the tremendous benefits that can accrue from initiating apprenticeship programmes, could secure a first-mover advantage for themselves from the same.

RECIPE FOR INDIA'S SUCCESS

As he puts it: **"Make in India is a good platform. Development is a key conclusion."**

When it comes to exacting the maximum benefit and leverage from manufacturing productivity, **a focus on the areas of Logistics and Infrastructure development is paramount**.

For exports to increase, ports should be developed; otherwise it discounts the profitability of goods made cost-effectively. Other related areas, which need to be developed are warehouses and godowns; to meet the requirements of sufficient capacity to store goods, and speedily push them on their way to foreign lands where they are needed.

Furthermore, essential raw materials and other inputs for industry, including power and coal, should be readily available at economical rates. This would also be a major factor in enhancing the global competitiveness of Indian industries.

THE QUALITIES OF A 'SUPER CEO'

A final few words of advice from Mr. Kriegner to aspiring leaders and CEOs:

"A CEO should essentially be a **straight-forward person**, and **should not play politics**. He should be **humble** and be **willing to learn**. He should provide frequent and open, **transparent feedback** to his people to enable their development and progress. He should be able to **manage people** effectively and be capable of **having an honest, open dialogue with them**. Also, he should be **ethical in his approach to professional matters**. But most importantly, he should have the **vision** to be able to see the big picture and **implement it all the way down the organisation**."

Mr. Kriegner has indeed encapsulated the essence of leadership and the role of a CEO role in a nutshell.

> **"** *Providing a balance between work, family life, private life, social interactions, as well as an element of spirituality are key essentials to generating a feel-good factor* **"**

-MARTIN KRIEGNER

Human beings are essentially social beings and love to experience and provide care and compassion.

Based on this foundation, **'WORK-LIFE BALANCE'** should be given priority by leaders so that the stress experienced in the rigours of the day-to-day working environment gets reduced, and the individual is rejuvenated and refreshed.

This allows the individual to think creatively rather than mechanically, and also enables him to lead a complete life, giving his best at work and at home.

RAMESH
HIRANANDANI

CHAIRMAN
R HIRA GROUP
OF COMPANIES

> ❝ *We believe that charity begins at home, so our employees are given top priority, and we extend to them financial help for the education of their children and provide medical assistance, whenever and in whatever form required* ❞

-RAMESH HIRANANDANI

The philosophy of businesses should be primarily people-oriented. People within the organisations are the true ambassadors for the brand they represent.

A true leader is a 'people's-person' at heart. He looks into the human capital engagement as one of the key areas for his organisational success.

Unless the function of Human Resources is given the same importance as the functions of Marketing and Finance are given within an organisation, the organisation will always lag behind its human-resource oriented competitors in the long run.

Thus, wisdom lies in establishing an organisational culture wherein employees get nurtured and evolved and are motivated to give their very best at all times.

S ince this is a global era, we simply had to include one dynamic CEO located outside Indian shores in this book.

And who better to suit this role than Ramesh Hiranandani – the Chairman of R Hira Group of Companies headquartered in Dubai – **Hira Industries having ranked among the 10 best SMEs in Dubai in 2013 by the CEO of Dubai SME, Government of Dubai.**

That is indeed a rare honour, and it would be interesting to note how a new age CEO from a foreign land leads his organisation.

The Hira Group consists of 14 companies, with operations spreading over India, Africa, the Middle East and the AGCC countries.

They are experts in setting up state-of-the-art air-conditioning and ventilation segments for leading institutions such as hospitals, 5 Star hotels, engineering plants, commercial and residential complexes, and also the Dubai Metro.

A DYNAMIC CEO WHO PUTS HIS EMPLOYEES WELFARE AND DEVELOPMENT FIRST

Ramesh, a qualified Mechanical Engineer from the prestigious V.J.T.I., Mumbai, is a **hands-on CEO who continuously develops new methods and systems to enhance the quality of products and services to ensure progress, growth and customer delight.**

Ramesh does not just focus his energies in expanding his already substantial customer-base, but is actively involved in ensuring his employees are well trained and that they advance professionally by organising special technical seminars where they can hone their skills.

He is also interested in ensuring his employees improve their lifestyles and achieve a healthy work-life balance.

CLEAR VISION AND
EFFECTIVE IMPLEMENTATION

When asked about his organisation's corporate values, he enumerates that Hira Industries is dedicated to providing customers in the construction sector with products of the highest quality, by forging successful partnerships with them, exceeding their expectations, and gaining their trust through outstanding performance by every member of the Hira Industries team.

He also ensures the provision of a work environment where employees can meet their potential and thrive in an atmosphere of professionalism.

The aim of Hira Industries is to become the **'Employer of Choice'** within the Building Supply Industry in the IMEA (India, Middle East & Africa) region.
An excellent Vision, and one which aligns perfectly with their Corporate Brand Perception, which is to focus on Quality and Excellence in all that they do.

WHEREVER POSSIBLE, 'GO GREEN'

S ince the 'hot topic' of the decade is CSR, we asked Ramesh about the CSR initiatives of Hira Industries. In this regard, their thrust is on multiple areas.

In Ramesh's words: "Corporate Social responsibility is the commitment of the Group and this starts at the top with the Chairman. I can say with pride that all our Group employees remain totally involved with welfare activities for the society and the community."

As Ramesh puts it: "CSR runs deep in the Hira family."

He continues: "The Hira Group of Industries regularly devote time and money to environmental sustainability programmes, alternate energy/cleantech, and various other social welfare initiatives which benefit employees, customers and the community. A major effort with which every Group employee is involved is to introduce the **GREEN EFFECT** wherever possible."

BLESSED ARE THOSE WHO GIVE

"We believe that charity begins at home, so our employees are given top priority and we extend to them financial help for the education of their children and provide medical assistance, whenever and in whatever form required."

Hira Indutries also extends financial help to NGOs in India which are involved in helping cancer affected patients and cancer survivors. They also provide financial assistance to charitable hospitals which carry out cataract operations for needy villagers in rural areas.

These are indeed noble initiatives and we complimented Ramesh on the same. He humbly responded that these initiatives provide immense inner satisfaction to himself and other shareholders as well as their families. Truly, Ramesh is a smart leader blessed with a heart of gold.

As though the above were not sufficient, Hira Industries proposes to enter another area of CSR, which is to provide financial aid to a new initiative launched by NDTV India to provide a special 'portable lighting system' to villages in India where power connections are non-existent. He said his organisation proposes to support this cause on an ongoing basis to ensure that less fortunate citizens can live comfortably.

CHOOSE 'INCLUSIVE GROWTH' OVER 'INCOME DUSTRIBUTION SCHEMES' — THEY WORK BETTER IN THE LONG RUN

We asked Ramesh for his views on **'Inclusive Growth'** and on this subject he had a **unique perspective.**

"The inclusive growth approach takes a longer time perspective to achieve, as the focus is on productive employment rather than on income distribution, as a means of increasing incomes for excluded groups. Inclusive growth is, therefore, supposed to be inherently sustainable and distinct from income distribution schemes which are a short-term measure to reduce the disparities between the poorest and the rest, which may have occurred on account of well-intended policies meant to jump-start growth. So while income distribution schemes can allow people to benefit economically in the short-term, it is inclusive growth which allows people to truly contribute and partake in overall economic growth."

INDIA WILL SURGE AHEAD IN THE GLOBAL ARENA

And Ramesh sees good hope for India, his motherland.

On his vision of the 'India of the Future,' he is thoughtfully optimistic and says he believes that India will have a growth-oriented economy under the present Government.

He adds that he will not be surprised if the GDP of India touches double digits in the next three years, or at least before the next general election.

THE THREE MOST IMPORTANT ATTRIBUTES THAT A CEO NEEDS TO DEVELOP

And ultimately, the all important question which we posed to Ramesh – 'What three crucial traits do you believe a CEO should possess in this modern business environment?'

The answer, according to Ramesh, is thought provoking.

He says, "In **Yoga**, we learn that **'CLARITY OF MIND'** brings in **'CLARITY OF THOUGHT AND IDEAS'** which results in **'CLARITY OF ACTION.'** The net result from these three attributes is progress and growth."

Thank you Ramesh, and may your organisation grow to greater heights with you as its guiding force, and may we see your vision of a developed India soon come true.

> **" Clarity of mind brings in clarity of thought and ideas, which results in clarity of action "**
>
> -RAMESH HIRA

Clarity is a very important word in the dictionary of leaders.

Clarity leads to commitment, and therefore a good leader constantly thrives to bring in clarity of thought, which he then clearly communicates to his team and workforce.

This helps in the enhancing the factor of resonance.

Ideas begin to resonate in the mind-space of employees, thereby making the 'impossible' goals possible and achievable.

In the world of action, leadership thought takes the most primary of seats. Therefore, it is of utmost importance to see how thoughts evolve with ideas and get implemented through actions by a conscious workforce.

Truly, clarity is the beginning of all that is good and great in the world of leadership.

AYAZ
MEMON

CEO Insight

> **As in life, so too in sports, some leaders can be intuitive, while other leaders derive their strength form a foundation of strong experience**

-AYAZ MEMON

INTUITION is one of God's gifts given to mankind. We may call it the development of our sixth-sense, but for a leader who consciously practices the art of leadership, intuition plays on his reflective mind.

At the same time, **EXPERIENCE** is also a valuable commodity, for it confirms the pattern of action towards a particular situation or circumstance.

Ideally, both intuition and experience are essential ingredients in the recipe for leadership success.

Why have we included Mr. Ayaz Memon (a successful leader in his own right in his chosen field) in a series of interviews about successful CEOs and their views on corporate leadership, and corporate functioning?

Quite simply because he is a veteran sports journalist and author, having covered major international sporting spectacles for over three decades, and specialises in cricket reportage. **In India, successful performance and leadership in all spheres is often related with victory on the cricket field (even headlines in financial newspapers often scream: 'The Sensex Hits A Sixer').**

And Mr. Memon through his unique position to offer close insights into this sport, brings out a veritable bouquet of flavours of the personalities who comprise this 'Gentleman's Game' at the apex level and the leadership and performance styles of its key personalities and the elements which drive the players to scale greater heights with each passing season. **So Mr. Memon is a man in the unique and happy position of offering keen insights to CEOs on leadership from the perspective of cricketing greats.**

He regales and also simultaneously enlightens us as he speaks at length on the attributes of the various cricket captains who he was fortunate to be able to interact with from very close quarters.

Which is why we have reserved this 'special treat' for our leaders towards the end of this volume on leadership.

188

THE CORPORATE CEO AND OTHER LEADERS CAN LEARN A LOT FROM SUCCESSFUL CRICKETING CAPTAINS

As in Life, so too in Sports, some leaders can be intuitive; while other leaders derive their strength from a foundation of strong experience. Who is the more effective leader of these two? The answer is always visible in the victories that are achieved and the success which resonates long after the game is over.

The game of cricket is very like business in many ways. In fact, it is often said – **'Business is a game.'**

By gaining insights into the mind-sets of successful cricket captains who have led their teams to victory against strong opposition, in the most competitive of environments, with the pressure of the entire nation's eyes watching, a lot can be profitably learned by corporate CEOs and leaders.

The similarities between cricket and business are sufficiently striking, and what Mr. Ayaz Memon has to say on the subject of leadership will be of great value for the corporate world.

CEOs NEED TO HAVE A
'DEGREE IN PEOPLE'

O ne of the examples he provides is that of former England cricketer and captain, **Mike Brearley, a clinical psychologist and psycho-analyst by qualification and training.**

After he had initially retired from the game, he was requested to reconsider his decision by the English Cricket Board to once again don the England cap and captain the demoralised English team who were struggling 0-2 down in the 1981 Ashes Series against Australia. **As a result of Brearley's electrifying presence and captainship, England subsequently went on to win the Ashes that year.**

After this stunning comeback, which was made possible by Brearley's astute leadership, this is what **Australian fast bowler Rodney Hogg** had to say in admiration of a worthy opponent: **"Brearley has a 'DEGREE IN PEOPLE,' and he knows how to derive the very best from his team."**

A CEO'S PRIME JOB IS NOT TO PERSONALLY PERFORM, BUT TO LEAD

As Ayaz Memon puts it: **'There are kings, and then there are king-makers.**

Brearley was cast in the mould of king-maker. A modestly average player, in today's age where runs and wickets appear to matter more than psychological motivation, he most certainly would not have been made captain, but he definitely knew how to lead his team to success.

He captained the English international cricket side in 31 of the 39 test matches that he played in, winning 17 of them and losing only 4; a very successful winning percentage.

ALL GREAT PERFORMERS NEED NOT MAKE GOOD LEADERS, AND VICE VERSA

In contrast to Michael Brearley, Ayaz Memon mentions the example of Ian Botham (also of the England cricket team), who though a very good performer, was not effective in his role as captain of the side.

As a captain Botham did not succeed, his failure leading to the lowering of his personal morale and spirit, and subsequently affecting his performance. But Botham as a player flowered under the captaincy of Brearley.

Brearley's leadership and motivational genius brought out the best talent in Botham to the fore, and Botham blossomed into a one-man army and a match-winner. In fact, so impactful was Botham's performance to the ultimate result of the 1981 Ashes, that the series itself is now known as 'Botham's Ashes.'

Though the performer was Botham, the transformation of Botham into a match-winner was attributed to Brearley and his leadership style.

This is when the phenomenon of 'Leadership' in cricket; being people oriented, i.e. getting the best out of your team members, became widely accepted as a very important role in itself.

A DIFFERENT STYLE OF LEADERSHIP –
BUT EQUALLY EFFECTIVE

Then Ayaz Memon goes on to speak about another very successful and talented team in cricketing history – **the West Indies team under the leadership of Clive Lloyd.**

The West Indies team, under the towering and fatherly-figure of Clive Lloyd was an indomitable side, even winning the first two cricketing World-Cups with ease.

But once Lloyd retired, no other captain (with the possible exception of Vivian Richards), has managed to bring out the best in these talented and volatile West Indian individuals and lead them to glory.

HAVE CONFIDENCE IN YOUR OWN ABILITIES AND IN THOSE OF YOUR PEOPLE

Another example of a strong cricketing leader that Ayaz Memon uses to illustrate his point of leadership playing a determining role is that of **Imran Khan leading the Pakistan cricket team.**

Ayaz Memon observes that while Brearley was a thinker, a strategist, a mind player; Imran Khan led from the front, and led with aplomb and tremendous charisma.

He would only ask people to do what he could do himself, and then proceed to demonstrate by doing it better than anyone else on the team.

Mike Brearley and Imran Khan – Two vastly differing leadership styles, but both succeeding superbly in their own right. Thus the leader needs to be aware of his strengths and play to them.

Imran Khan would take big risks because he had tremendous self-belief in his own ability to turn around a situation if it appeared to be getting out of hand. The risks he took almost always paid off. His sense of conviction led him to always think and act positively, both on the field and off the field.

Once, during the course of a Pakistan v/s West Indies match, (West Indies was then rated the best team in the world), and the match was being played in Pakistan, Imran Khan had insisted on having Indian umpires for the game so that no one could accuse him of home umpires being partial to the team after he won against the mighty West Indies.

194

This was the level of confidence he had in his own leadership abilities and the skill and talent of his side.

Later, when India played Pakistan in Pakistan, he similarly had umpires called in from England. (This was the series when Sachin Tendulkar made his test debut.)

Thus it was Imran Khan, owing to his tremendous self-belief and positive thinking and risk-taking appetite who is credited with introducing the concept of neutral umpires into the cricketing system.

Imran Khan can definitely be considered a visionary, which is also one of the essential qualities of a great leader.

A GOOD LEADER ENSURES
SOUND SUCCESSION PLANNING

Another parameter of sound and visionary leadership is the ability to observe and identify leadership skills among the next-in-line; a concept which is known in the corporate world by the term 'succession planning.'

Again, in this regard, Ayaz Memon explains how this particular leadership quality was demonstrated by Imran Khan. During the 1991-92 World Cup (which Pakistan won due to Imran's lead-from-the-front brand of leadership), Imran had slightly shifted focus and was now driven more by the zeal to build a cancer hospital in the memory of his mother.

Touching forty, he was slowing down, no longer the fearsome batsman and deadly fast bowler that he was in his prime. But he was well aware that if he didn't continue to wield the baton, the chances of Pakistan winning the coveted trophy were slim.

This was the time when Imran looked at developing the next rung of cricketers to take over the leadership position once he left. **This was the period when he identified Wasim Akram and other fast bowlers and groomed them to take over in the role of performers as well as leaders, wherever they appeared to fit best.**

GREAT LEADERS SACRIFICE PERSONAL PAIN FOR THE GOOD OF THEIR ORGANISATION

I mran Khan, according to Ayaz Memon, was surely among one of the all-time cricketing greats. He led ably by motivating his team, and he had the ability to inspire, and lead not necessarily as a thinker and a strategist (which he was very capable of doing), but also with zeal and passion.

In the 1982-83 series when Imran was the captain, the Pakistani team led by him played against the Indian team which was led by Sunil Gavaskar. Both teams appeared equally matched and well balanced, but Imran Khan was in such great form, that he got forty wickets in the series and demolished the Indian side.

More important, later on in the same series, although Imran had injured his ankle and was advised rest, he insisted on bowling, to inspire and to lead, to ache in silence for the good of the team and in pursuit of glorious achievement.

This demonstrates the hallmark of a leader for whom his team or organisation is paramount – to sacrifice personal pain, perform to the best of individual ability when the team or organisation needs it most, thus putting team before self in a glorious display of superlative leadership.

LEADERS SHOULD SELECT PURELY ON MERIT FOR THE GOOD OF THE ORGANISATION

Further espousing Imran Khan's exemplary qualities of leadership as a case-study and object lesson to aspiring leaders is learning from the case of Majid Khan, thirty-six years old, a veteran of the Pakistan cricket team, who was close to breaking a world-record. Imran, who was otherwise a dictatorial leader and insisted on selecting only the best talent in his team, permitted Majid Khan to play on emotional grounds (although Majid was not in very good form), so that he could attempt to break the record.

But unfortunately for Majid, Kapil Dev (the Indian bowler), was in devastating form and got Majid Khan out for a zero in that test. Although the decision appeared debatable, Majid was given out by the umpires. This was an era when there were rest days between the five days of a test match. On the rest day of that match, General Zia ul Haq, the then President of Pakistan, held a banquet in honour of the two teams, and during the course of the banquet asked Sunil Gavaskar, Kapil Dev and Syed Kirmani (the Indian wicket-keeper), if Majid was really out. Haq had pledged to ensure Majid would play the next match if the umpires had made a mistake in their decision. But Kirmani reassured Zia that Majid was really out.

Then it was that Imran and Haq ensured that Majid did not get to play again, falling just short of what would have been a world record.

The lesson for leaders here being, even if it is a question of family, when in a professional environment, a leader should never compromise by selecting anyone but those whom they believe to be the best to have a place on their team. (Majid Khan is closely related to Imran Khan, both being first cousins.)

LEADERS NEED TO TAKE QUICK YET CORRECT DECISIONS

A yaz Memon then goes on to relate leadership on the cricket field with leadership in the corporate world.

In sports, especially in cricket, how a leader performs; how a team under that leader performs, is instantly visible to those watching the game in real-time, and the leader's performance is immediately analysed, evaluated and dissected.

The difference between leadership on the field and leadership in organisations being that in the organisational context, **it takes a little longer time for observers, stakeholders and analysts to see the impact that the leader's tactics, thought processes, decision-making capabilities and actions have on the success and productivity of his team and the organisation.**

The kind of on-the-spot decisions a captain makes on the cricket field (not snap-judgments but quick yet well-thought-out decisions when speed of decision making is of utmost importance), is a technique that can also be mastered with practice by a CEO/leader in the corporate arena. To this extent, that decisions in the corporate environment also need to increasingly be taken faster, yet correctly, is a parallel between the cricketing world and the corporate world.

A quick assessment of the opposition's/competition's capabilities and weaknesses, assessment of abilities of one's own team players, analysis of the prevailing eco-system; all these ought to enable the leader to think and move fast, which is essential when competition is fierce as it is today.

IDENTIFY FUTURE LEADERS
BASED NOT JUST ON PERFORMANCE,
BUT ON LEADERSHIP ABILITIES

Another keen observation that Ayaz Memon makes is that **a dressing-room in the cricketing world is representative of a microcosm of an organisation**. Fifteen talented and ambitious individuals of varying temperament, personality types, ways of functioning, is very similar to the type of team that a CEO needs to effectively lead in the corporate context.

And in the corporate environment too, one needs to develop succession plans, just as in the world of cricket. Generally, the consistently best performing player usually ends up being the vice-captain, and once groomed, takes over as captain in due course of time.

In the Indian cricket team, when Bishen Singh Bedi was the captain, many future captains secured valuable experience as vice-captains under his tutelage: they included Sunil Gavaskar, Kapil Dev, Ravi Shastri and Dilp Vengsarkar.

An important point to note while identifying future leaders is to bear in mind that great performers by default need not make good leaders. **This could be clearly seen in the case of the 'Master Blaster' Sachin Tendulkar. Sachin was undoubtedly a great performer but failed as a leader when given the opportunity to captain the Indian side.**

EVERYONE HAS CERTAIN WEAKNESSES – A GOOD LEADER OVERLOOKS MINOR WEAKNESSES IN HIS PEOPLE AND FOCUSES ON THEIR STRENGTHS

Another insight on leadership which Ayaz Memon brings out is that **one of the valuable qualities a leader needs to develop is the ability to incisively and extensively understand the individual capabilities of the key players on his team and devise overall tactics accordingly to play to their strengths.**

In the case of Sachin Tendulkar, or for that matter even Brian Lara of the West Indies, (both extraordinary players but ineffective as leaders) – one of the primary reasons for their not being effective as leaders was that they expected too much from their team members.

They always felt that if they were personally putting in long hours at practice sessions and eliminating their personal technical weaknesses by sheer effort, why could the others on their team not do the same.

Due to their individual brilliance and single-minded dedication to the game, they became intolerant of even the minor weaknesses of the individuals they led. Such an attitude of perfectionism sounds good on paper, but in practicality it creates an environment ripe for fear and for friction. The friction may not be visibly exhibited, but it is always in the mind and becomes a key source of disruption and underperformance.

A GOOD LEADER IS
ALWAYS APPROACHABLE

Sometimes the most unexpected individuals make for excellent leaders and captains. This is why current leaders need to keep their eye open to spot leadership talent, for it can come from the most unexpected of quarters.

Take the case of Kapil Dev who came from a small town in Haryana. He made for an excellent captain, leading India to World Cup victory in 1983 against the apparently invincible West Indies. What made him a success?

It was the sheer honesty of his raw communication, his skill and passion for all departments of the game, his ability to inspire individuals to put in that extra effort for his sake, and most of all – his down-to-earth nature which made him **approachable** by all concerned.

LEADERS, BE ALERT –
AVOID COMPLACENCY

Ayaz Memon advises that a factor which leaders should always steer clear of is the element of **complacency**.

This is something that has often led to the downfall of many a good leader and his team.

Take the case of the West Indies in the 1983 World Cup finals against India. India had batted first and had posted such a low score that when the West Indies' turn came to bat, they relaxed and took it easy. Subsequently, and fortunately for India, the West Indies batting line-up collapsed due to their early complacency and they were bowled out for a score even lower than that which India had posted.

This 'loss' to apparently weaker competition due to complacency is observed a lot in the corporate world too.

As just one example, most of the top 10 companies of 1975 are not around anymore.

A leader needs to be continuously alert, keenly sensitive to environment changes; and constantly upgrade himself and his team with up-to-date knowledge and modern techniques to meet challenges from all sides.

THE CRICKET-BASED MODEL FOR CORPORATE LEADERSHIP

We were fortunate to have Ayaz Memon share with us a cricket-inspired module which he has developed and which he uses to train individuals on how to systematically build a strong career-path or train organisations how to beat their competition and rise to best-in-class.

This module is based on six types of strokes which are used by batsmen in cricket in different situations and to face different types of deliveries from different categories of bowlers.

What follows is Ayaz Memon's Model in brief, containing the six strokes in cricket and their appropriate usage, linking the same to leadership in a corporate context.

STROKE NUMBER ONE – FORWARD DEFENSIVE (LAYING THE FOUNDATION)

Forward Defensive Stroke (Related to 'Laying Foundation' in Corporate Leadership):

The learning for corporate leaders from this stroke is **how to protect your domain and your bastion.**

The philosophy of this stroke is to be used in the corporate environment when initially laying the foundation and defining the boundaries of your organisation and the scope of its activities.

On the cricket pitch, this is demonstrated by batsmen tapping the crease; knowing and firming their ground when they initially come out to the crease at the beginning of their innings.

STROKE NUMBER TWO – COVER DRIVE (ACCURACY)

Cover Drive (related to '**Accuracy**' in Corporate Leadership):

In corporate terms, this comes through confidence acquired after the initial groundwork is done and the foundation is sturdily laid.

The leader has to identify the gaps and loopholes in the competition's field placements and has to accurately hit the ball through these gaps.

This stroke helps you score 'quick runs.'

Mastering this stroke helps you gain market share in segments of the target audience which are left untapped by your competition.

In the corporate context, here is where you generate quick revenue and high margins of profitability.

If you find that the 'gaps' through which you aim to hit are not getting you the necessary 'runs,' it is time to change the direction of your initial strategy and lay a fresh foundation.

STROKE NUMBER THREE –
LEG GLANCE (IMPROVISATION)

Leg Glance (Related to '**Improvisation**' in Corporate Leadership):

The great India batsman Ranjitsinjhi (Ranji) invented this stroke many years ago.

He could play this difficult stroke with ease, as he (and many Indians), have supple and flexible wrists.

With this stroke he was able to sweep the ball into **unexpected territory** whereas the English batsmen with their wrists stiffened by their cold weather could not play this stroke and merely hit the ball in standard fashion in front of the wicket.

This stroke, says Ayaz Memon **illustrates the need to dominate the competition by innovating in areas where you hold the advantage.**

STROKE NUMBER FOUR – THE HOOK SHOT (DOMINATION)

The Hook Shot (Related to '**Domination**' in Corporate Leadership):

This is all about sheer aggression.

The Hook Shot should be attempted when you are so confident in your team's talents, abilities, your USP, your competitive advantage, that you are willing to take that extra risk.

As a leader, once you have done the hard work of laying the foundation, once you have creatively improvised and identified and developed your USP, now is the time to play the hook shot and score an organisational sixer.

STROKE NUMBER FIVE – STRAIGHT DRIVE (TIMING)

The Straight Drive (Related to '**Proper Timing**' in Corporate Leadership):

This shot looks easy, but can be played successfully only with skilled hands.

It looks relatively easy to play, but is not as easy as it looks to the observer.

Master batsmen such as Gavaskar and Tendulkar used this stroke quite often and profited from it.

It is all about perfect timing.

In corporate life too, a successful leader is one who not only knows how and what to do, but more importantly, when to do it.

Playing this stroke well with the right timing results in the joy of – 'minimum effort – maximum output.'

STROKE NUMBER SIX –
THE SWITCH CUT (DISRUPTION)

The Switch Cut (Related to '**Disruption**' in Corporate Leadership):

Kevin Pietersen, normally a right-handed batsman, often changes his hand position mid-way through a stroke and temporarily adopts the stance of a left-handed batsman, confuses the bowler, and hits the ball for six.

The lesson here for corporate leaders is to disclose to no one your crucial moves before you make them.

If you master this skill, you gain the advantage by disrupting the status quo and moving ahead while others are left standing.

CHANGE TACTICS AS PER THE SITUATION

A yaz Memon then explains that captainship in cricket is a little different from captainship in other team sports.

For example in hockey or in football, the bulk of the strategising is done and the tactics for the game are worked out **before** the captain leads his team onto the field.

But in cricket, even an over of six balls can have six different tactics demonstrated (one for each ball); and the captain, the bowler, the vice-captain and other members of the team often have mid-field discussions after every ball at crucial stages in a game.

This is a lesson for corporate leaders; that they should involve their key team-members in crucial decision making, and that tactics need to be changed as per the situation.

MOULD YOUR LEADERSHIP STYLE TO FIT YOUR PERSONALITY AND YOUR ORGANISATION'S UNIQUE NEEDS

Ayaz Memon elaborates that captaincy is not a one-size-fits-all phenomenon.

Every successful captain follows certain basic principles, but also evolves his own style and develops tactics which work for him and his team to get the best results.

For example, Sunil Gavaskar was quiet and diplomatic in his approach to leadership, whereas Kapil Dev, equally successful, brought his own natural aggression into play in his leadership role and it worked well for him.

This too, should be borne in mind by corporate leaders – not to copy a successful leader's style, but to build your own according to your unique personality type and the needs of your organisation.

LEADERS USE EMOTIONAL APPEAL TO GOOD ADVANTAGE TO IMPROVE THEIR TEAM'S PERFORMANCE

A yaz Memon also observes that sometimes a leader has to deliberately provoke a player to get the best out of him.

He says that inspiration need not come from the individual leader's words or actions alone, but a sentimental act or an emotional appeal can often get the message through in the healthiest manner.

As an example, **Steve Waugh**, when he captained Australia at the onset of the new century, inspired his team by getting everyone to wear the style of caps worn by the Australian team in the year 1900 (a hundred years ago), thus arousing fond nostalgic memories of their team-mates from a bygone era. This spurred the team to perform to greater heights in memory of their team-mates gone before, and can be considered as **'Inspiration by legacy.'**

For **Wesley Hall** (the West Indies fast bowler), his captain **Frank Worrell**, used the power of emotion to goad him to bowl the team to victory. Worrell motivated Wesley Hall to pull out all his reserves of strength and skill as his people were depending on him. Worrell told Hall, **"Do it for your race, do it for the Black people. Make them proud."** Wesley Hall then bowled like a man inspired.

LEADERS NEED TO CONSTANTLY COMMUNICATE THE 'VISION' — THE BIG PICTURE

So these are the scintillating examples and anecdotes which Ayaz Memon regaled us with to drive home the point that a CEO or a leader in a corporate environment can and should learn a lot about the art and science of successful leadership from the great captains of the cricketing world.

Just how do leaders make an apparently ordinary individual perform at extraordinary levels? Quite simply, by **constantly communicating the 'Vision' – the message of a higher purpose.**

When this is done regularly and repeatedly, the leader's thought process begins to resonate with his team-mates and the individual team-members begin to identify themselves with the message of the common vision driven home by the leader.

People can be motivated best if they are able to see the big picture.

SELECT LEADERS TO HEAD DEPARTMENTS AND STRATEGIC BUSINESS UNITS AS PER THEIR 'FIT'

With 'change' being the corporate buzz-word today, there is a lot for the corporate leader to learn on this vital aspect as well from the game of cricket. Cultivating **'Change-Champion Leaders'** throughout the length and breadth of the organisation is an art which CEOs need to master, if an organisation is not to be left behind its competition.

Cricket today has evolved as rapidly as has the corporate world, and various forms of cricket such as Test Cricket, One-Day Cricket, 20-20, Six-A-Side, and many others are being played almost simultaneously.

Though the basic rules remain the same, vastly different leadership styles and skill-sets are required to succeed in these different formats.

Thus one may need different captains leading the same team in these different formats, with even a few players changing according to the needs of the format.

This is because the leadership thought-process, the strategy and tactics, and the player temperament required for a test series is vastly different from that needed to succeed in a one-day match.

Corporate houses too, need to identify leaders with specific temperaments and skill-sets and utilise their services where they would create maximum positive impact – for domestic markets, global markets, front-end customer roles, back-end administrative roles, some suitable for marketing and others for sales, and so on.

GREAT LEADERS AND GREAT WORDS ON LEADERSHIP

Lastly, we requested Mr. Ayaz Memon to choose those according to him were the top cricketing captains of all time.

It is a difficult choice to narrow so many great captains down to a small number, but he gave us the following list of names – **Frank Worrell, Imran Khan, Mike Brearley, M.S. Dhoni** and **Sunil Gavaskar** were the best ever.

And as he puts it, **"Leaders are not defined by the colour of their skin, or inheritance and legacy, nor by their educational qualifications, but by their success in the complex art of understanding the game they play and the way that they deal with and bring out the best from their team players. Ever optimistic, the great captains and leaders rush forward to meet and master every single challenge that comes their way."**

> **"** *One of the hallmarks of a leader for whom his team or organisation is paramount – is to sacrifice personal pain, perform to the best of individual ability when the team or organisation needs it most, thus putting team before self in a glorious display of superlative leadership* **"**

-AYAZ MEMON

If the 20th century was the age of individualism, the 21st century can be termed the era of teamwork.

Here, the team leader proves the bonding factor that brings the team together to perform extraordinarily.

To lead is also to sacrifice, and great leaders go to any extent to suppress personal pain and ambition to fall in sync with team goals and organisational objectives.

THE LEGACY OF THE CEO

The world is remembered by the impact and impression left behind by leaders in every walk of life.

CEOs too, as leaders of the corporate world too will add their personal charisma and human touch to the organisations they create or run.

People are loyal to people: this being the established fact, it is crucial that CEOs are able to create a succession of leaders to enhance and carry their thought process forward.

It is at the highest level of thought that the leader considers himself as a mere trustee in an organisation and runs the set up with all humility.

In this manner, the CEO's personal brand gets aligned and merged with the organizational brand.

In the age of Internet and social media, the CEO's image which is created in the market space plays a vital role in how customers view the enterprise. The impact of his thoughts, words and actions will be the foundation on which organisations of the future will build their pillars of success. If the right leader is not chosen, then organisations will hit the dust and soon wither away into oblivion.

To establish the legacy he leaves behind, the CEO must meticulously engage himself into the methods and habits which would build and strengthen the character of his organisation. This character will make him adored and admired in the eyes of his workforce, which will in turn establish internal loyalty and inner employee branding.

All this will then reflect on the outside eco-system; namely the customers, suppliers, outsourced agencies, and so on. This in turn will establish the aura across his brand, which in turn will leave behind a heart-warming experience.

Thus when we studied brands that have lasted over at least 50 years, we observed that an experience with these brands left behind a human touch which lingered long after the purchase and consumption of the product or service they represented. This emotional component distinguishes a brand from a commodity. **And it is primarily the job of the CEO to ensure this emotional connect becomes part and parcel of the brand he leads.**

Let us conclude on a focused as well as a philosophical note; by unraveling the LASER Focus that is so essential to sustain and propel the organisation into the future:

L – Your organisation should constantly follow the LURE Principle – to learn, unlearn, relearn and through market experience go back to the dashboard. This induces and encourages the innovative spirit across people, product and processes.

A – Adaptable to constant change that is taking place in the market. The organisation should be nimble-footed and alert to context. This should be:

      -On the economic front
      -On the socio-cultural front
      -On the trend and technology front

S – Settle fast into a new environment with minimum stress and adjust gracefully to inevitable change

E – Enrich self and organisation with knowledge as one is part of the century of knowledge and also become wise with experience

R – Resonate in tune with the internal and external eco-system

---

With all the above fulfilled, the CEO is on the march to leave behind him a trail of legacy and a source of knowledge, making his organisation eternally appear in the Golden Book of Great Enterprises.